Angel

S. N. Montoya

S. N. MONTOYA

First Edition, 2022

ISBN-979-8-9863977-2-6

EireneBros Publishing LLC
4414 82nd St, Ste 212, -318 Lubbock, TX 79424
www.eirenebrospublishing.com
www.facebook.com/EireneBrosPublishing/

Dedicated to my love, for always inspiring me and never giving up.

S. N. MONTOYA

Chapter One

The Girl with the White Wings

When everyone saw the small, white, feathery wings clinging to my back, fear struck their faces, the fear of the unknown, and the fear of what I could do. A baby has never been born like me before; I didn't know that at the time, but I was soon to learn. I simply thought they were surprised by my amazing beauty and fast growth rate. I truly realized I was different by how many tests they did on me. It was nearly impossible for them to jab needles into my skin; when they did, it healed right away. It hurt more when they plucked my delicate feathers, and those took a lot longer to grow back. The tests never seemed to end throughout the first few months of my life, and every single one just felt like pain.

The first few years of my life were spent in a very secure environment. I hardly ever got to see my mother. My life was mainly full of many different faces arguing about what they should do with me. She told me never to worry, though, as the people working with me were only trying to understand what I was and what I may become. Part of me found that hard to believe.

"I just don't know what to do with them. They stay pretty clean, but I feel like I need to brush them or something...what about shirts?

I don't want to ruin them, but at the same time, I don't want to stuff her wings up in them because that would tangle up the feathers or make some fall out." These are a few of the many questions mom had about me. Eventually, we figured out that cutting the shirts and lightly combing my wings was the best way for both of us.

As I grew older, my skin became tougher. Doctors could no longer puncture it with any needles. They had to stab into it with a knife just to give me medicine that I supposedly needed every now and then. It only hurt for a brief second, and then the pain subsided. They had many problems with this, though; my wounds come close to instantly healing on contact. Everyone began to worry about why a child would have such skin, which seemed only to get stronger by the minute. Many doctors asked themselves if there would come a time when nothing could puncture me. Would that make me the most indestructible human alive? Although, that wouldn't really make me human at all.

I was released from the facility around the time I turned five years old. I later learned a secret military base ran tests on "gifted" individuals. They tried to do their best to understand how people similar to me came to exist. They concluded that I must stay hidden from the world. Still, to develop as normally as possible, I lived with my real family. I would later learn, however, that they genuinely did not care.

We live in a relatively small house, surrounded by acres of dense forest. Mom said that we did not have a single neighbor, the closest one being about ten miles away. She said that this was one of the government's conditions for letting me come home. I was, after all, supposed to be hidden from the world.

She never let me outside of the yard, so the house was the only thing I really knew with time. I could tell my mother struggled to cope with having a daughter stuck at home constantly. She would get aggravated easily over the little things, such as my constant wing shedding. I had two other siblings, both of which were normal in my mom's eyes. I would wrestle my brother, Jake, within the house and leave trails of feathers everywhere. Mom wanted everything to be clean, so we often got yelled at for roughhousing. She never seemed to be as mad at Jake, though, but he wasn't the one with wings.

My sister, Emily, gets treated with much more respect than the both of us combined. She is the eldest, so she often got stuck at home watching me when mom had to go to town. Jake usually tagged along with her since she didn't have to work due to the government funding us. But Emily did not seem to mind taking care of me; she is usually level-headed and knows how to deal with my burst of energy and playfulness. Emily is ten years older than me and often reminds me of a gentler version of mom. She has long blonde hair and dark brown eyes.

"Emily, do you think mom will ever let me go with them?" I ask her, staring out the window as mom and Jake pull out of the driveway.

"I don't know," She sighs. "I think you will have to wait until the world is ready for you." She places a hand on my shoulder. "But do not worry so much, little sis. You are safest here anyways, and I will do my best to entertain you." I hold onto her words. I have always hoped that one day I would be able to freely leave like everyone else, but she tells me that it could be a dangerous place for someone special like me.

"Can we go outside now?" I ask her, knowing that mom won't be back for a while. She gives me a slight nod, prompting me to excitedly jump off of the couch and towards the back door. We often spend our time alone out in the forest, exploring and enjoying nature. It's the only place I feel truly free.

As soon as I step into the sunlight, I stretch my wings out as wide as they go and let out a happy sigh. Emily follows behind me, pulling a hoodie over her head. I don't feel the cold as much as she does; it has never bothered me, at least. I start walking towards the tree line about ten yards from the back door without a word.

"No, you should try to fly again today." She says, making me stop in my tracks. Fly? My head goes back to the first time I tried to propel myself into the air, and it ended in a face plant.

"Do I have to? What if my wings aren't made for it? Humans don't fly." I reply, still thinking about the last attempt.

"Yes. In case you haven't noticed, humans don't have wings. But you do. You can only get better." She says rather sternly. I let out a sigh, and squat down a bit, fully extending my wings. With a big push of my legs and a strong flap, I rise about a foot before landing back on my feet.

"You have to give it more effort than that; you're not just jumping, you know." She says, ignoring my worried expression. I try once more, jumping and flapping as hard as I can. I get about three good thrusts in this time until I realize that I am about five feet in the air with nothing holding me. With a shriek, my wings fold in, and I fall into the grass with a soft thud. My eyes met Emily's, her face in her hands as she tried to hold back a laugh.

"A girl born with wings who is afraid to fly," She chuckles. She continued trying to make me fly that day but to no avail. The thought of it always scared me. How could I trust two feathery things attached to my back to keep me in the air? I would dread the day I ever reached the clouds. Eventually, she did seem to understand my dilemma, and we began to spend our time alone just exploring the forest without trying to fly. But despite my differences from her, she made me feel as normal as she could.

Jake was a whole different story. He is only a year older than me but much taller. Mom says he has dad's blue eyes, but he died before I was born, so I had to go off what they told me about him. Although he doesn't like the woods, he is fun to play with. We usually play with his dinosaurs and action figures. Sometimes we go outside and pretend to shoot each other with stick guns. Mom disapproved of guns much and had to tell me that I am a lady, not a boy, but we found ways to hide it from her. However, I would rather play with guns and dinosaurs over dolls and makeup kits.

As the years went by, I continued to be secluded from the rest of the world. Every day, I would watch my siblings get on this big yellow bus that would take them away for most of the day. I longed to know what it would be like, to actually go out and meet people. But the ever-growing wings on my back seemed to get in the way of everything a normal kid was supposed to have. Sometimes I wished I was not so different and wondered what it would be like to go to school and make real friends. Men in fancy uniforms would often show up to the house and talk to mom and me. They asked me many questions, like how I felt and if I ever felt the need to harm other people. I do not know why they would ask such things, as I could never see myself hurting another human being.

"Come on, sis, let's play a hunting game," Jake said one day, running toward the backyard. I followed, puzzled that he would want to play a hunting game. He hates the woods. But I followed him anyway. "It's called Cheetah and Gazelle; I have played it a few times at school."

"What is Cheetah and Gazelle?" My ten-year-old self asked. He simply laughed and told me it was really simple. One person is the cheetah, and the other is the gazelle. The cheetah has to try and catch the gazelle and bring it to the ground. We have never played games involving animals, so it sounded kind of interesting.

"You can be the cheetah first since you're so fast. Now, just think cheetah thoughts and give me a ten-second head start." I thought of the graceful cat, the intense speed it can reach with its four fragile legs. It would be amazing to be a cheetah and run as fast as my legs could carry me, absolutely free. Jake runs off, happily giggling. One.

Without much warning, swirls of green start to come from the ground and make their way around my body. Two. It's as if the spirits of animals run and dance around me, chasing each other and playing in the green that is starting to cover everything within sight. Three. I could barely see my brother through them as he circles the mass I was now trapped in. I try to scream, but nothing comes out. Four. My body is suddenly forced to the ground, tingles covering me from head to toe. Five. I land down softly on four paws. Six. Claws emerge through the fur on each paw in a smooth and oddly relaxing way. Seven. A tail extends from my spine, and black spots appear throughout my fur. Eight. My teeth grow sharp points that make them stick out of my mouth. Nine. My vision becomes much clearer, and my hearing improves significantly. Ten.

Once the swirls are gone, my brother nearly faints. A young, winged cheetah cub stands only yards away from him, wings tucked tightly to her sides as she shakes in fear. He slowly steps back and begins to shout.

"Mom! Come out here quickly; sissy turned into an animal!" His words make me cower down and let out a weird cat-like whine. I look up at his scarred face, still shouting for mom as his eyes begin to water. I stare hard at the ground, flexing my claws and grinding them into the dirt. A strange feeling emerges from within me, almost as if I had just drank a very large energy drink. A great sense of strength overcomes me. I leap around my brother without much thought, feeling overwhelmed with new energy. My wings pulse on my back, begging me to take flight. The idea breaks my energy surge, and I notice him watching me with fear in his eyes.

"Stop it! It's me! I don't know how this happened, I swear!" I say to him as mom comes out the door. Her hand covers her mouth as she sees me shaking wildly on the ground, completely unsure as to what I should do or how this could even happen. Jake runs up to her, saying I tried to attack him. Instead of a dirty look, a hiss escapes me, showing off my sharp cat teeth. I instantly retract myself, flatting my ears as if trying to apologize. How is this even possible?

"Where is Angel?" Mom asks, looking around for me. I tilt my head at her, *'are you that dumb? It's your daughter....'*

"I'm her mom! I don't know what happened! We were playing a game, and I turned into this thing!" I growl, making her back up a little bit. What is happening? I don't mean to growl, but it happens. I don't mean to hiss, but it just comes out as if on some sort of natural instinct.

"Don't call me mom, and don't call me dumb! I'm not your mother. I did not give birth to some freak!" She is shaking now. I flatten my ears farther and cower down as a green tear slides down my fur. She starts to pace back and forth, keeping Jake behind her. But how did she know I called her dumb? I could have sworn that I only said that inside of my head.

"Mom..." I let out a cry, slowly stepping towards her. She backs toward the house and pushes Jake inside as slowly as possible, with a long, depressed-like sigh. She hesitates before turning her eyes back toward me.

"Get in the car, Demon; I will be there soon." She snaps as Emily comes screaming out of the door, her hands balled up into tight fists. My heart sinks.

"Mom! She is your daughter and my sister! You can't take her; she is just a kid!" She cries, coming up to me as if to snatch me up, but freezes at the sight of a cheetah cub struggling to open the car door. Emily's face isn't fearful like theirs were. She looks at me with a softness and slowly walks towards me. I manage to open the door with my jaws and jump into the car.

"Angel, what happened to you?" She puts a shaky hand on my back as I lay my head in the seat. I ignore her. I'm not a human. I don't belong here. As much as it hurts, mom is right. I am not a part of this family. No one here has green eyes and wings. I don't know if anyone does. Maybe I am a demon after all. My sister's touch soothes me only the smallest amount, as I can only think of what could possibly happen now.

"Get back, Emily." Mom shoves my heartbroken sister away from the car and away from me. She throws a bag at my feet before slamming the door with a loud bang. Emily backs away slowly, tears covering her face.

"You'll be in so much trouble for this," Emily's eyes never leave me as the engine starts and mom steps on the gas. I still sense her eyes as we go down the road and away from home. It felt as though my heart had been ripped right out of my chest. She is the only one in my life that has cared for me with all her heart. I had thought Jake did too, but it takes a very strong person to look over the fact that someone is entirely different from everyone else, possibly even dangerous.

That was the last day I had with my family, the first day I found out what I really was. I am no human. I am a demon sent here to only bring destruction and wreck everything around me, even if my intentions are not so. Is there any other reason for me being around besides this one thing?

Mom took me far from home, flying past many stop signs and streetlights. The city changed into a few houses here and there as we sped along, farther and farther from home. It was hard to make out many details as she continued to push her foot on the gas, making everything blur together. The tears covering my eyes didn't help much, either.

After what felt like hours, we finally stopped. We were in what looked like a neighborhood, which was odd considering I had to be hidden. We sat in silence for a while, mom's breaths turning from rapid to deep. She closed her eyes and sighed.

"I am sorry, Angel. You will thank me for this. Now that you have changed, it is time for you to go to a new family that can handle you and leave us behind. We will both be safer this way. I think the woman supposed to take you lives around here somewhere, but I don't have time to look. Now please, make this easier on the both of us and get out."

She didn't shed a single tear as I hopped out of the car and grabbed my bag. She disappeared into the night and left her daughter forever. I thought I meant more to her than this, but I guess ten years of living in the same house and leaving feathers everywhere can change a person's mind. I wonder what she meant by saying that the person supposed to take me should be around here? How would I find said family, and would I want to?

Chapter Two

Abandoned

A small bench in the middle of a small park ended up being my home for many days. I ran through the supplies in the bag within the first week, it wasn't very much. There were crackers, a couple peanut butter and jelly sandwiches, and a water bottle. Rain offered me water, but no food ever came my way. I didn't know how much time I had or how long I could keep hiding from the kids and adults actively visiting the park. Would it be better if they found me and killed me? That'd make everything so much better. I was nearly on the verge of doing it myself until I learned how to shift back into my regular, winged self. Once I did that, I realized how skinny and starved I was, seeing many bones in my tiny body. My wings even seem drained of whiteness and look almost grey. I knew I needed food, and soon. The thoughts of stealing someone's food from their house struck my mind. That may be the only way to get some food into my system, even though it is against the whole "Angel" part of my name. Maybe I really should switch it to Demon.

So, going against my name, I try and plan a way to steal some of the pizza I smell within a blue house not too far away from me. I tuck my wings into my sweatshirt and smooth out the lumps before walking towards the house. Young children scatter everywhere, so I figure it shouldn't be too hard to quickly take a slice and run off with it.

Watching the children play makes me think of my brother, how often we would wrestle together in the house. What I would give to be back there, letting him tackle me to the floor even though I was much stronger than him. I shake the thought out of my head, remembering he was part of the reason I was here, driven by hunger to steal.

As I scan around the house, I notice only a couple of angry adults chatting in a corner as they barely keep an eye on the swarm of kids. A young girl eyes me carefully as I walk up to the fence. With her eyes still following my movements, I slowly walk along the side of the fence towards a large picnic table full of pizza. The smell makes my stomach feel sick, and I nearly vomit, but I hold it together as my mouth begins to water.

"You look funny." She says, curiously watching me put a finger over my lips as I reach down for a warm slice. She doesn't yell or shout for anyone; she just watches me as I casually walk off with some of their food.

After I know I'm safe, I take small bites, so it doesn't upset my aching stomach any more than the smell is. I nibble on the slice, trying to savor every bite before it disappears. My stomach still urges me to find more food as it is practically starved, but I ignore the feeling as best as I can and figure it would be best for me to get some rest now. I lay quietly down on the bench as tiny raindrops hit my forehead. The trickle of water from the sky soon turns into a flow as a crack of thunder sweeps the sky, forcing me under the bench with my wings over my head, saving me from the downpour. I am soaked and shivering within just a few minutes as more thunder and large and bright beams of lighting shoot from the sky.

My eyes shift to a large tree near the playground; its large branches call me. I crawl out and run towards it with what little energy I have left. As I reach the base, I let my body fall onto the damp grass, covering myself with my wings.

I thought the storm would never end, but after it started to get light out, the rain stopped, and so did the thunder and wind. I uncovered myself from the safety of my wings to see trees and branches covering the road. A large branch from the tree now laying only a few inches above my head, the end of it dug into the soft ground.

I slowly crawl out from under the tree and make my way back towards the bench in an attempt to search for my bag. It sits a few feet from the bench, lying in a small puddle. I grab one of the straps, making my water bottle fall out of a new hole. I let out a sigh and throw them both in a trash can before making my way back underneath the tree branch.

I don't know how much longer I can live out here like this. One of these days, I'm going to end up being hit by a car or blown away by another immense storm.

Chapter Three

Justin

"Hello? Are you okay? Hello?" A boy woke me from my nap. I slowly open my eyes but don't move. "Where are your parents?"

"I don't know. They left me." I say weakly, lifting my wings up a bit, realizing I forgot to hide them in my sweater due to the storm. He looks at me with confusion and sorrow, but his eyes instantly brighten at the sight of them.

"You have wings! Your family left you because of that? Grab my hand; I'm going to bring you to my mom." He says, grabbing me tightly without objecting and pulling me out from under the branch. The movement sends a dizzy spell over me. I pull back on him, not sure if I should go.

"Where are you trying to take me?" I huff, trying my best to keep my feet planted on the ground. He tightens his grip on me, determined not to let go.

"To a warm place with food. You need it." He says, sounding much more like a command than a suggestion. I let out a soft sigh and let him pull me away from my tree.

We slowly make our way to a big, brown house near the edge of the forest, at the very end of the neighborhood. The green grass seems inviting, but the thought of entering a stranger's home makes me feel cold inside. I don't know these people, so why would I stay in their home?

The white door pops out from dark brown, giving the house a nice contrast. The inside is even nicer. White carpet fills the large and open living room. Leather furniture sits around a large flat-screen TV next to a weird box that must be for music. Many speakers hang up high around the room for a lot of audio that I didn't think anyone would really need. I begin to panic; I am cooped up in this charming home that is near perfect. I am almost guaranteed to destroy something, and it will more than likely be expensive. The sooner I am out of here, the better.

"I'm not sure about this..." I say, grabbing the door handle as fast as I can. His arm quickly tightens around me, and he pulls me away from it. I have a feeling that my inhuman strength will be useless without having any energy, but I'm determined to try. I thrash around as he holds me, doing my best to wiggle free from him. His grip easily holds me as I am too weak to fight back, so I begin to slap him with my wings, being the only thing he seems afraid to touch.

"Mom! I need your help, please..." He says in the doorway, holding me in place as I fight very weakly to get away. I give him a hard kick in the side that barely does anything as a woman quickly runs into the room, freezing at the sight of me. Something about her looks oddly familiar as if I have seen her face before. The distraction makes me stop struggling and attacking him with feathers.

"What's going on? Oh my. Angel?" She asks, looking at my sad green eyes. I nod my head, realizing she is one of the doctors who cared for me in my earlier years. I notice Justin's distraction and twist his arm quickly, making him release me with a shriek. I fling the door open and descend the porch stairs, footsteps following me. Pain shoots throughout my legs as I go. There is no way I can outrun them in this state. The wings attached to my back catch my attention, and I realize forcing myself to fly might be the only chance I have right now. With a small jump and a weak flap, I rise a couple feet but fall back down and hit the ground as my wings give in. Everything quickly spins around in a fast blur of color, followed by darkness.

"She is awake," Justin says as I open my eyes. I stare at the white ceiling in the living room, lying on the comfortable couch. I quickly rip a wet rag off my forehead, only to put myself in pain.

"What's going on?" I ask, sitting up. Before my question is answered, a plate is handed to me, with chicken and mashed potatoes on it. I quickly gobble it up before asking any more questions. The only thing more important to me right now is warm food, according to my stomach, that is.

"Angel, you need to tell me what happened to you." His mom says, sitting next to me on the couch. Since I know I'm stuck here, I decide to tell the not-so-strange woman what has happened. I set the plate down on the glass coffee table and start to explain the long story in a languid and troubling way. She doesn't seem to like any of it either, shaking her head at many parts and cursing under her breath, something she assumed I did not hear.

"You're a shifter! I suspected as much, truthfully. But I can't believe Tracy did that; she will surely be punished." She retorts, dialing a number on the phone. I quickly grab her hand before she can finish. The person she is calling is either a police officer or my mother. I can't deal with any of that at the moment. I just want to rest in peace.

"I'm not going back! No way! I don't want to ever see her face again, please!" I start to cry. She jerks her hand away and puts the phone up to her ear anyways.

"No worries, my darling, I won't ever let that happen." I nod my head and sit, taking a deep breath. My eyes meet Justin's, who is angrily rubbing his arm and staring at me with a glare.

"Hello, Tracy." My heart sinks, and I try scrambling for the phone. I am stopped by an even angrier Justin. "Nothing new, besides the fact that a very skinny and sick child is laying on my couch as we speak, her beautiful white wings all gray." She pauses. "One bag of food? She has been on that bench for three weeks! You know you were supposed to bring her to me! The child is only ten! What the hell were you thinking! I hope you know you will never be seeing her again for as long as I live and...hello? She hung up on me!" She angrily hangs up the phone and walks out of the room rather loudly.

"Can I just go now?" I say, heading toward the door once more. Justin quickly jumps in my way, seeming annoyed.

"All we are doing is trying to help you. If we wanted to hurt you, we would have. Be thankful for a change." He gives me a slight shove back. I shake my head at him.

"I am thankful. But you don't want me here! I know you two won't hurt me, but I might hurt you. I will tear this family apart just like I did mine. I am a demon." My voice shakes at my last words, and I go back to sitting on the couch, with no emotions to feel. He slowly joins me, speechless. We sit in silence for a while, neither of us knowing what to say.

"That's not true; your mother was the one who wasn't strong enough to handle you turning into something amazing. None of this is your fault." He finally breaks the silence. I let out a yawn and lay my head on a small couch pillow, not sure what to say to him. "You can borrow my bed if you want; you still seem pretty tired." He smiles. I slowly sit up and nod as he stands and walks down a hallway. It is full of colorful paintings and pictures of Justin and his mom. I start to wonder if his dad died just like mine did... The end of the hall leads to a small room with a stone fireplace and a ceramic tiled floor. A white sofa sits near a table and a bookshelf. In the center of the room, a spiral staircase leads up to another room, which must be Justin's. The staircase feels as if you're walking on air, as the steps are held together by clear beams. His room is all dark hardwood flooring with dark blue walls. A queen-sized bed sits on the far wall in the center with a Batman bed set.

"Thanks," I yawn, happily jumping into his bed and enjoying the amazing comfort it has to offer. It's been a long while since I have been in a bed, let alone one as soft and comfortable as this one.

Once I wake up, I am still in the comfortable Batman bed, but Justin is nowhere to be seen. I take a slight glance at the window just feet away from me, tempted to escape. My mind drifts to the last time I was on my own. I starved. I cannot go back to how things once were. I'll have to make things work here. It will take a while, but it seems like all I have is time and no other place to call home.

Footsteps come up the stairs. The door opens, revealing his mom, who smiles at the sight of me. She must have expected me to try and escape like I had debated so many times already. A plate with two pancakes loaded with butter and syrup is in her hands. I sit up and thank her as she hands it over to me.

"Did your mother ever tell you that the government had a plan for you in case something went wrong?" She sits on the end of the bed as I take a few bites of the warm and delicious food. I am finally beginning to feel satisfied by my hunger.

"I don't want to go back home," I say between bites, "They would make me feel out of place."

"Home is the last place you'll end up, my dear. I work with the government, and believe it or not, I am the person your mother was supposed to take you to. We haven't seen a shapeshifter in years but suspected that you might be one," she says.

"She told me that she dropped me off close to your house; she never told me why there was a plan for me to be with a different family, though...please do not tell anyone you have found me yet..." I trail off, wondering why I was not meant to stay with the family I once thought loved me.

"Two days is the best I can do," she states, grabbing the plate from me and then telling me to take a shower and wear the clothes she laid out at the end of the bed.

Once she is out of the room, I walk over to Justin's bathroom and undress from my old, nasty clothes.

It smells like an air freshener, and a towel is neatly hung on a rack next to the shower. It isn't too hard to operate; turn the knob one way it's hot, and the other is ice cold.

The clothes she left are way too big, so I easily tuck my wings inside without being uncomfortable. I'd rather not cut holes in someone else's shirt; it just doesn't seem right. When I come out of the bathroom, Justin is sitting on a black bean bag chair in front of a large flat-screen TV with an Xbox controller in his hands. He notices my presence and pauses his noisy game.

"Mom said you didn't try to escape last night," He looks over and laughs at the baggy clothes with a mushy mass on my back. "That's a good thing. Why not cut the shirt like you did with your other clothes?" he asks.

"These are not mine," I shift my wings around in a more comfortable position. "They are also too big for me, so it's not all that bad."

"Well, those are some of my mom's old clothes. She won't mind if you cut holes in the shirt." He pulls out a pocketknife that makes my eyes widen a bit. "What? I stole it from my dad before he left," he says, turning me around and carefully cutting slits in the shirt. I slowly maneuver my wings through the slits and reach back to pull them the rest of the way.

"I could have helped," he says after watching me struggle through the process.

"It's fine. I can do things on my own." Before he can object, his mom comes through the door.

"I have to run to the store. I'd take you with me, but if you are seen, well, that would be a problem. I'm going to hate leaving two children alone, but I'll be back as soon as I can. Love you, Justin." She speeds off down the stairs and right out the door. My mom would have never let me stay home alone. She always made sure Emily was around to keep an eye on me. I guess his mom has more trust than mine does or did.

I watch Justin play the game, unsure of what to do. *His mom mentioned 'other' shifters, so would that mean more people like me?* I think to myself, comforted by the possibility.

"Your mom said I am a shifter. Does that mean she has seen others like me?" I ask him, breaking the silence.

"No, but she had told me about a time when there were some. It was before she was born, I think. But if you're a shifter, what can you shift into?" he asks, his voice turning to an excited tone. I smile at him, slowly moving away from the game and thinking my cheetah thoughts as I did once before. Tingles start to course through me, and the light green swirls around. The strange thing is, it's not nearly as many as last time. I don't lift off the ground but stay firmly planted where I am. Justin stands himself up at the sight of a cheetah in his room.

Energy begins to surge through my body once more, turning my weak and gray wings back to their fluffy white selves. I stretch my legs out in front of me, yawning at the sensation.

"I told you! I am more than just wings," I start to say as he stares at me with amazement, quite the opposite of what my family had shown me. "The first time I did this, there was so much green and swirls...and now it was barely anything, and I changed so fast," I say in a voice a little different and deeper than my own. Instead of backing away and running like I had expected him to do, he comes closer and holds his hand out to me.

"Are you soft?" He asks just as he gently touches the top of my head. His touch makes the feeling inside me intensify much more than it already was, making me want to run and jump around like a crazy person. "Wow, a real shapeshifter."

"Am I?" I ask him. He slowly nods as he strokes behind my ears. After a few more scratches, I back away from him and leap around the room, trying to get rid of all the energy now surging through me. It is as if my body is being rejuvenated. My effort barely cracks the surface, making me run and leap even faster, avoiding the obstacles in my path, so I don't ruin his room.

"Easy! You're gonna explode!" he laughs as I start to slow myself.

"Impossible...I think!" I laugh as I stop before him. He reaches out for me, but I jump to the side and roll, giving him a playful stare.

He smiles and lunges at me, but I easily pounce, making myself glide right over him, and he lands on the floor with a thud. Before he can recover, I jump on his back and lay down so he can't get up. He sighs and puts his hands flat on the hard floor.

"You sure are playful as a cat," he says, rolling over, making me fall off. I shake myself and run in front of him. "Your eyes, so green!" He pokes my pink nose and stands up. Still unable to hold the happiness in, I jump onto his bed and bounce on the softness. He ignores me as best as he can and looks out the window.

"Maybe we could go to the forest; it's only just through the back-yard. It's a big one too, goes for many miles," he smiles, putting a water bottle in a bag. I don't hesitate to follow him down the steps and out of the house. The moment my paws leave the door and hit the soft grass, I take off in a run, moving my legs at a breakneck pace. Energy surges throughout me as I pick up speed, feeling un-stoppable as I move through the trees. It felt as though I had been resting for a long time, eager to finally use the energy.

A large maple tree catches my attention, stretching high into the air. I leap onto it, extending my claws and running up it. They make it very easy to grip the rough bark and pull myself up the trunk. By the time I reach the top and bottom four times over, Justin appears panting on the ground. Maybe humans aren't as good with speed as me. I hop down from my branch and greet him with a ragged breath. Running so much has even caused me to tire.

"Used all your energy?" He says as he opens his water bottle. I shake my head and circle him, trying to prove I've still got more kicking. "You are so fast. Gone the moment you hit those trees." He laughs as he finishes up the water bottle. Someone was very thirsty. I stand up as high as I can on my four legs and stretch my wings out proudly.

"The fastest!" I laugh.

"Well, how about we walk to the house now?" He slowly turns back toward where we came from and starts off. I let out a sigh and decided it best to join him in his stroll in my normal form. Although it had only been a day, my body was back to normal weight and color.

Once we return, his mom is already home, and she is waiting silently on the back porch for us. She rises at the sight of us, then looks us over as she opens the door for us to come inside.

"If she was seen," she starts angrily, her eyes slightly bulging at the sight of my now white wings. Justin quiets her with his finger, making her place her hands on her hips.

"We snuck into the forest to get all of her energy out. She would have torn my room, then the whole house, apart!" He laughs. I nod slowly from behind him. She lets out a loud sigh and tells us to go upstairs and clean ourselves up. I didn't notice how much dirt covered my body, along with Justin's. Traveling through the thick woods at a fast pace may not be the brightest idea…

Once we go upstairs, he guides me to yet another bathroom in the house that's off of a room full of cardboard boxes and old trinkets. This bathroom isn't as big as his, but it is still bigger than what I'm used to. He hands me a towel and walks off into his room without a word.

My hair is a tangled mess; it looks as if it hadn't been brushed in a long while. My eyes glow bright with green as they always do, and tiny shimmers of green swirl around in them, giving my eyes an alien-like appearance.

After the shower, I check to see if Justin is in his room. When I see he isn't, I walk down the steps to find him arguing with his mom. I clear my throat loudly, so they know of my presence. They instantly stop talking, and I am greeted with a plate of fish and chips. They remain silent as we eat our food, but the tension is high, so I speak up.

"May I ask what that was about?" I look into Justin's eyes, waiting for an explanation.

He hesitates before answering, "Well, my mom over here called the government and told them that she found you. They are going to come here in an hour to talk to you about what you want." I shrink at his words. '*I had one more day*! *This isn't fair*!' I yell to myself as I look at Maggie; her face gets red with anger.

"Stay out of my head! Now you just sit on the couch and wait for them to arrive. If you behave well, I will forget you took such a tone with me." She gets up and walks off to her bedroom with heavy footsteps.

'*But I didn't even know I was in her head.*' I try to reach out to Justin.

'*It's* okay; I talk to her like that a lot. Just try and remember not to think so loudly because your power is strong.' He answers me.

After waiting silently on the couch for about fifty minutes, a loud knock echoes throughout the house. Fixing my hair, I get up and open the door to see a tall man who's going bald in the head. The gun strapped to his belt makes me shiver; however, his bright smile reassures me that I've done nothing wrong.

"I can sense the fear in you," his strong but soft voice says as he sits on the couch next to me. "But you have no need for fear; this is all to help you. Now, can you tell me what happened that day?" He takes a pen and a small pad of paper out of his pocket. I've never written anything before, but as I watch him write, it doesn't seem very hard at all. And so, I explained to him what happened; how I first discovered my animal form and that right after she threw me on the curb.

"Uh-huh...I see..." He said every now and then as I answered his questions and explained what it was like here in this new home. Once I said I was finished, he quietly shut his notepad and then leaned in close to me. "It seems if you do not want to go to a facility again, that this environment may be a permanent home for you. If this is alright with Miss Monroe, she could adopt you and call you her own." He then gets up and goes into Maggie's room as I sit there, shaking. Justin quickly appears next to me.

"You mean, I might have a sister? Be an older brother?" He smiles. I clench my fists into tight balls and sit back on the soft cushions of the couch. His look quickly changes from happiness to worry.

"You don't want to have a new family...do you?" A sigh escapes him.

"I do, but it's just so fast. I feel like only last night I was in my own bed with my mom reading me my favorite bedtime story, my sister yelling at me for breaking one of her dolls, and my brother...oh, how I miss him..." My words are drowned out with tears. Justin's arms instantly embrace me in a comforting hug, which I gratefully accept. I try to speak once more, but I am immediately shushed by his finger, gently pressing it against my lips to keep me quiet.

"You can still visit your family, well, your brother and sister anyway. Can you tell me what they are saying in there, with that hearing of yours?" I shake my head. I know I could very easily listen in if I tried, but I feel like that's an invasion of their privacy, so I just continue to soak his shirt with tears as my answer.

After sitting on the couch for what seemed like forever, his mom and the official walked out of the back bedroom. I wipe my tears away as fast as I can as the man thanks her for her time and leaves the house quietly.

"Looks like you may be my future foster kid if everything pans out smoothly," Maggie says, sitting in a white chair across from us.

"What if I don't want to be adopted?" I protest.

"You may not want it, but you need it, Angel. I'm sorry, but you don't have anywhere else to go. Plus, we had already somewhat arranged this. We will do our best to provide a safe environment for you." Her words silence me as she continues to talk about how we will make this work the best we can.

She explained that the department of defense had assigned her to me not very long after I was born. She was to be my guardian if I lost control of myself or if my mother could no longer care for me for some reason. This is a much better alternative than me being taken back to a government facility and having my childhood taken away from me, she stated rather confidently. Part of me wondered what Justin was thinking about all of this. Had his mother even told him? Why is she so special to be the one to take care of me?

She also explained that we would have to go to court with my mother and a few government officials to figure out her punishment and decide if I am still not a threat to the environment, given my recent developments.

Maggie made me sleep on the couch while we cleaned out the guestroom. I didn't mind it too much. Sure, it's not as comfortable as Justin's bed, but it's much better than my old one. It took us about two weeks to fully clean the room and set it up for me to live there. During that time, Maggie and I got closer, and I slowly began to gain her trust, as she did mine. Justin had most of it, but I still could not fully trust him yet.

"She's a good mom. One you can count on." Justin told me when we were finishing making my bed. I nodded my head in agreement as I answered him:

"She's better than mine."

Chapter Four

A New Family

"Angel, are you ready?" Maggie asks from downstairs as I finish combing my wings. We are about to go to court, which none of us are too excited about. The thing I dislike the most is how we have to dress up. I hate dressing up so girly; it's just not something I've been used to. Justin hates dressing up, too. He was fighting his mom the whole time she was putting a nice black shirt on him. At least he doesn't have to wear a stupid dress that shows all of his skin.

I take a quick look at myself in the mirror, my dirty blonde hair flowing past my shoulders and partway down my back, covering part of the plain blue dress that went just past my knees. It seemed modest enough to cover my shoulders and come up just below my neck. It showed a large portion of my back, a hole big enough where my wings could safely extend out of it. There would be no hiding them today. The more I looked into the mirror, I realized how different I looked. Even Emily did not look so mature at my age.

"Ready as I can be," I call to her, making my way down the stairs.

The car ride to the courthouse is tranquil, as everyone is far too nervous about what happens next. I'm still not sure if I want to be adopted, but I know this is better than going back to the government. Who knows what kind of environment they would keep me in. Part of me wishes to learn to fly and get far from here.

We soon arrived at the courthouse, nervousness in me rising with each and every step. I nearly collapse as I walk through the doors. There are so many faces that I do not recognize that are all staring at me. The judge is an older-looking woman with tiredness and determination in her eyes. Almost all of the people inside have guns strapped to their waists and slightly edgy looks. Maggie and Justin sit down in the front row, leaving me standing staring face to face with the judge.

I hold my head and wings high as I walk down the aisle, trying my best not to look intimidated by all of the men around me.

"Hello, Angel," she starts in a quiet, gentle voice. "I am Judge Clearwater, but you may call me Leah. Today, we are only here to talk about what happened that day and figure out what to do with the defendant, your mother. Will you please explain to me what happened on the day that you left your family?"

"I did not leave my family. They left me." I object. "And, what happened was..." I tell them everything, from when I shifted, and mom took me on a long car ride away, all the way up to now. Many people seemed excited by how I 'transformed' into a cheetah and asked me to show them. I start to shake at all of the shouts, not sure how to calm myself down, and Leah raises her hand for them to be quiet.

"Well, will Mrs. Star please come forward and tell me whether or not your daughter was lying to us, please?" The judge asks in a voice that didn't make that 'please' sound like much of a question. My heart sinks as my ex-mom gives a hard swallow and steps up to the stand, her figure seeming tinier and more pale than usual. Coldness fills me at the sight of her, still wondering how someone could leave their own child.

I look over at Emily, who must have been watching me the whole time because our eyes instantly meet. Tears fill both of our eyes, and I look away, wiping them away best I can before anyone else notices. I did not realize how much I missed my sister until now. She mouths the words 'I love you' before turning her attention back to mom. Jake is sitting next to her, his hands clenched together tightly in his lap as he watches mom, never once glancing in my direction.

"Well-I can't deny that I did indeed leave her, but I did make sure she had food and-"

"A small portion! That's all you gave her!" Justin's mom interrupts, followed by a pound of the hammer.

"Yes, there was only one bag, but I expected she would ration well; she is a smart girl after all. And I was just so...afraid. Her transformation caused me to panic." Mom's voice was starting to shake along with her hands. A small line of sweat was forming on her forehead. "It is unnatural, a young girl turning into an animal. I believe her to be something rather sinister." The judge seems furious at this but calms herself before speaking as best she can.

"So, you are admitting that you dumped your ten-year-old daughter on the streets with very little food and no shelter? Even though you were clearly informed that if anything went wrong, you were to take her to Miss Monroe?" She nods her head very slowly, not making any eye contact with the judge as she stares very nervously at the carpet, making me almost feel sorry for her.

"I was just so scared. I was worried that she might hurt me or someone else. It felt much safer to leave her on the streets than dumping her on someone else." She chokes.

"That, my dear friend, is a violation of your contract, not to mention you let her sit there for three weeks. If Miss Monroe had not come along and helped the poor girl, she'd be dead! And who are you to call a child sinister?" She booms angrily. "Jury, please discuss whether or not to convict Tracy of Child abuse and failure to follow orders," she says, pounding the hammer and sending them off to a back room.

"Now that the jury is gone, Angel dear, would you please step forward and show us this 'cheetah' form of yours?" she asks in a gentle tone. I glance towards Maggie, asking for advice, and she gives a slow nod. I close my eyes and think about being a cheetah again with a deep sigh. With a few tiny green sparks at my feet, I am on all fours within seconds. My body is again filled with raw energy, but I try my best to keep calm and keep eye contact with Judge Leah.

"PUT DOWN YOUR WEAPONS!" Maggie shouts. My ears flatten as I look around at all of the terrified men pointing their guns at me. I lower myself towards the ground and let out a growl while extending my wings to make myself appear bigger. Judge Leah pounds her hammer, and the men slowly lower their guns.

"Now, now. Let us not scare her into not controlling herself, gentlemen. Angel, can you still understand me?" she asks, staring into my now glowing green eyes.

"Yes, your honor," I replied. An audible gasp comes from one of the men.

"How do you feel, in this animal-like form?"

"I feel like myself, well, as much as I can, considering I am on four legs," I reply, glancing towards my mother. I wonder how she feels now, seeing me up here, about to be taken from her. Her eyes drop, and she looks towards the ground, a stray tear swelling in her left eye.

"Do you feel like hurting anyone?"

"No."

"Can we all agree that she seems like the same person beforehand?" Leah asks, staring at the agents that surround me. They slowly nod, staring at me in disbelief. A cheetah with wings, talking in a courtroom. I can only imagine how confused they must be feeling. "Then, we can agree that she is no different than the other shapeshifters."

"Then, it is settled. Angel, as of now, I declare that you do not appear to be a public threat. This, however, does not mean that you will not become one in the future. We have seen shapeshifters like you before, but never with wings. "Maggie," Judge Leah stares directly at her, "you will give the Secretary of Defense monthly reports on Angel's actions and behavior to ensure that she is behaving correctly. Do you understand?"

"Yes, your honor."

"Then it is settled. You are free to leave. Case dismissed."

The court, of course, found my mother guilty, and now she will have to spend five years in prison. It seems to be a bit much. I mean, I know she deserves it, but she is still my mom, and deep down...I still care for her. And with her going to prison, it would be up to Emily to take care of Jake on her own. I noticed Judge Leah talking with Emily on my way out, so I was hopeful that she would be helping her somewhat.

But sure enough, I had a new mom. Justin was pleased about this; he didn't have any siblings to spend his time with, but that was about to change. I wondered what type of things the government would try to control within Justin's and Maggie's life now, though, since I would be living with them. Thankfully, though, we continued to live in the cozy neighborhood house so long as I would be able to conceal myself from the people living nearby. Hiding mainly consisted of staying indoors for as much as I could and sneaking into the woods where I could feel that same type of freedom I once felt at my old house with my sister.

Chapter Five

Growing pains

"How come your wings don't disappear when you turn into a cheetah?" Justin asks me one afternoon while walking through the woods behind our house.

"I don't know; they're a part of me. I think it shows that I am more than just a cheetah." I say to him, gracefully moving beside him on my four paws. I have grown quite fond of being this way; it was as though it recharged my body and filled it with life.

"It would be cool if you could hide them; that way, we could go on walks through the neighborhood." I let out a laugh.

"Even if I didn't have wings, I think seeing a boy walking his pet cheetah would be rather alarming." He nods his head in agreement, holding a stick in his hands as he ponders ways for us to be in public. Justin seems to like people much more than I do.

"What if you could be a dog? That would be easy to hide and pretty normal."

"What kind of dog?" I ask him, trying to imagine it.

"Hmm… it would have to be something small, that way, you don't scare away kids. But not too small. How about a golden retriever? Everyone loves those, right?" he asks.

I stop in my tracks for a moment, thinking of what it would be like to be a dog. It would be fun to walk about the neighborhood without having to hide. If I had thought of a dog first, would I have turned into one? It would probably have wings, too, so that would be a bust. I ponder, letting myself wish for a moment that I could be a golden retriever. It would probably be fun.

In an instant, my fur changes color slightly and becomes longer. My nose elongates and becomes more extensive. My claws extend out of my paws as they grow, and my tail becomes shorter and thicker. My wings retract into my body, disappearing into my fur and underneath my skin.

In disbelief, I looked up at Justin; I was now a golden retriever dog, four-legged and completely wingless. As I felt for my wings, I could still feel them, but it was as though they were dormant and protected within me.

"Your wings are gone, and you're a dog!" Justin exclaims, walking in a circle around me.

"They are still here, I can feel them, but they're hiding," I say to him, taking a few steps to get a sense of my new appearance. The amount of power I felt was much weaker than in my cheetah form as if I wasn't at my true potential.

Uncomfortable with my energy drop, I change back into my human self. I sigh with relief as my wings unfold from my body and make their appearance once more. As time went on, I learned that there were many different animals I could transform into, and often found it fun to experiment with Justin.

Once I accidentally tried an 'elephant' and broke part of the ceiling with my giant head. Justin's mom was furious, but she still let me stay with her. That's one of the things I love most about her; no matter what mistakes I make, she is always by my side, something I had never experienced before. She even kept it a secret from the rest of the government. As far as they knew, I could only turn into a cheetah.

Any animal Justin and I could think of, I turned into. It was pretty fun turning myself into a plethora of animals, but Maggie hated it. After a few months of me running through the house being every animal imaginable, she decided it was best that I did not shift while inside. Although I was upset with this, I understood. It probably isn't the best idea to have big animals running through the house any-way.

Justin and I spent quite a few weeks playing his Xbox 360. It was entertaining, and he hated it when I beat him at most shooting and fighting games, just because I'm a girl and am supposed to be bad at things like this. When we began to get bored of the games, we went and took walks through the forest and experimented with my strength and shifting skills. We found some unique things about me like I could easily tear a small pine from the ground and throw it like a stick and how I could see and hear things exceptionally far away. We played little games like 'telephone,' where I had to tell Justin what he said once he was across the forest.

I never tried flying again, though; I was too terrified of falling down and breaking my leg, or worse, my neck. Justin kept telling me that wasn't possible, but the fear kept me grounded for some time. I didn't care about the fact of how 'wings,' especially this size, always mean fly. I knew that I would have to try again sometime, but I wasn't really sure when I'd be ready or how I would know I was.

"You should try flying, just imagine it... Being up in the clouds, with no one to tell you what to do or how to act...so free." Justin said to me one day as we lay on the forest floor.

"What I imagine is me getting up super high then falling and hurting myself pretty badly." He just chuckled and continued to stare at the sky. Angrily, I rolled over and tackled him. He tried to fight, but my strength was no match for him.

"You weak human! Don't defy me!" I joked as he pushed with all of his strength to get up.

"How about we make this fair," I let him up, curiosity getting the best of me. He scavenged the ground, picking up two nearly identical sticks. "Swordfight."

Without much warning, he threw me one and swung at my side. I quickly reacted and blocked him, but he returned quick hits. He is pretty strong for an eleven-year-old but not strong enough. After a few easy blocks, I decided to go in for the 'kill' and knock his stick out of his hand, then put mine up to his neck.

"And... you're dead." I laughed as I dropped my stick on the ground. It was about time to get back to the house anyway.

We repeated these events quite often, going out into the forest and sparring with our stick swords. We eventually bought ourselves some fake wooden ones that were much more 'realistic' than our weak sticks. Near the end of the summer, Justin's arms were becoming much more muscular. One time, he outwitted me and actually managed to put his sword up to my neck.

Once school started for him, the days got a bit quieter. A lot of the time, it was just me sitting in my room and playing Xbox, or I would occasionally go out for a girls' day with Maggie. It was more boring with him learning human things that he would likely never need. However, these days, I started to become closer to Maggie.

"I wish you were allowed to go to school," she said to me one morning.

"I do not; the other kids would never consider me one of them. It's not worth it. I can learn everything that I'll actually need by experience, not by sitting in some classroom having someone tell me what to do," I argue, entirely against the idea of schooling.

"You learn some great skills in class, my dear," She then put a soft hand on my shoulder. "It does not matter what they think of you, but how you carry yourself." *Wise words, but I know all of the basic skills.*

Maggie looks into my eyes. "You really have to try and control your mind a little better; I'm always hearing things I know I'm not supposed to," she tells me.

"I learn new things about myself every day, but I keep forgetting to learn how to control that part of me," I reply. I now understand how my ex-mom heard me call her dumb a little more than before. However, is it even possible for me to control my thoughts and not let people listen to them? Never having my own thoughts wouldn't be good in front of people.

As the day went on, I sat up in my room and watched the movie "How to Train Your Dragon." It's a movie I've always loved. As the film goes on, I start to do small sketches of the dragons and accidentally shift into a dark blue dragon. Spikes start from the top of my neck, going all the way down to the tip of my tail. My scales are all black with a slightly blue tint. I barely fit into the room, but my ceiling is taller than most of the rooms in the house, so it's not affected by my massive wings that stretch out both far and wide. I haven't quite mastered the control of not shifting into the animal and/or creature I'm thinking of; it kind of just happens. One time I was sitting in a chair, and after a few seconds, it was just a pile of wood due to the tiny t-rex sitting on it.

I don't shift out of the dragon form right away but strut around, enjoying the power I feel from being a creature that was once just a fantasy. I try to keep my steps as light as possible, so Maggie doesn't hear me from downstairs; she would hate to find a dragon roaming around her house. I catch Justin in the corner on my last circle around the room, watching me with amused eyes. I immediately stop in my tracks and stare at him, glad the redness doesn't show in my scales. When did he get home?

"A dragon, eh?" He laughs, putting one hand on my pointed nose. "I am now a dragon trainer." I push him away with a claw, and a deep chuckle escapes my jaws.

"I was watching a movie and drawing...Then boom." I say as I wag my tail back and forth happily and admire myself for a few seconds. I accidentally knocked over a stand as my tail had begun to swing a little less controlled. Justin just laughs at me and picks it up as if nothing ever happened.

"Ooh, can you breathe fire?" He asks excitedly, opening the nearest window to me. I slowly approach it, feel the warmth inside my stomach, and find quite a bit of power to reach. I pull at it and open my jaws, releasing a stream of red-hot flames out of my jaws that slam into the dirt. The sensation causes a brief sense of panic throughout me, making me stop the flames abruptly.

"That's fricking awesome! You have no idea!" He runs a warm hand down my scaled back, which makes me tingle for the oddest reason, and then sits down on my bed as if it never happened. I shift back into my human form and sit next to him, feeling tired from using my power.

After a few minutes of silence, his hand slowly touches my left wing. I hold my breath as he runs it through the soft feathers. This is the first time anyone besides my ex-mother has touched my wings with allowance. I can feel the sense that his eyes are watching my face as he does so carefully, inspecting me to make sure I have no objections. Once I start to breathe again, he continues to feel through my feathers ever so gently.

"Sorry, I have always wondered what they felt like... They are so soft," he says. I reply with a yawn. "Did using the fire make you tired? If so, you should probably get some rest." He takes his hand off my wing and stands, uncovering part of the bed to let me slip inside the covers.

"Thanks," I quietly reply, still dazed by his hand on my delicate wing. Every touch I feel on them is amplified compared to the rest of me. Within minutes, I fall fast asleep and dream of his hand back on my wing, of the strange feeling it gave me.

I drift off into a dream rather quickly; I am running through the dark woods in my cheetah form, without a single person or thing in sight. But I don't feel alone. I feel myself skid to a halt. I scan around me, but I suddenly can't see a thing. Panic begins to overcome me as a branch cracks nearby. I freeze.

"Angel," the voice echoes. A strange yet calming, female one. "You must come to me, in the woods beyond your house..." she says. I try to speak, but nothing comes out. "Come." She repeats. My body snaps up from the dream, sweat covering my cheetah self.

Chapter Six

Midnight

"Do you ever get the feeling that someone is watching us?" I asked Justin the following morning.

"Not really, but I could see why you would. I mean… have you seen the wings you try so hard to hide?" he asks, trying to lighten the mood a little.

"Yes, but this is different. It scares me. I had the strangest dream last night...like something was calling me. I don't know if it means anything, though. It was just a dream, after all, right?"

"It could. Do you want to investigate?" he asks me.

"I don't see why not; it couldn't be anything bad… right?" We walk downstairs, greeted by Maggie making breakfast. Neither of us seems to be interested in eating, though.

"Now, you two don't get to go off into the forest without eating something first. Sit down," she commands, making us stop in our tracks. She never fails to put food in our bellies before going off on our outdoor adventures.

"What is it today, more sword fights?"

"No, just some exploring. You know how much I love the woods," I say to her, taking a seat at the table. Justin follows suit.

"Yes, just don't go too far. Even an angel could get lost in there. There are about ten thousand acres that way, you know. Wolves, bears, coyotes, cougars, you name it." I raise an eyebrow at her. "And, of course, a little girl that can casually turn into a dragon. Gotta watch out for her." She lets out a laugh. She has been surprisingly lenient about letting Justin and I explore the woods, mainly because that's the only way to enjoy myself. Plus, the deep wilderness tends to keep regular people out. One of the perks of living near the Dark Pines Forest.

"You saw that, huh?" I reply, wishing I had not been a dragon for so long.

"You shot fire out of the upstairs window, Angel," she smirks, setting a big stack of pancakes on the table.

After we finish our breakfast, Maggie lets us continue with our adventure. We cross the street, walking into the edge of the trees. The sounds of birds fill my ears, singing happily without anyone to disturb them. A distant branch cracks suddenly, and they become silent. I tried to focus on it; a lone wolf was stepping through the brush, just lengths from a deer. The sound sends it into a full-out run, forcing the wolf to leap from the shrubbery and go into pursuit. Their footsteps begin to fade as they move out of my range.

"What're you listening to?" Justin breaks me from my daze.

"A wolf, it was hunting its prey. I can't tell if it got it, though," I say, trying to hear it once more but to no avail.

"A wolf? I wonder how far away it is!" he says, a hint of fear in his voice. I don't answer, only thinking about how beautiful the wolf must look. I feel myself quickly turn into a silvery wolf, standing on four paws yet still taller than Justin.

"The only wolf you should fear is this one," I say, beckoning for him to continue walking into the woods.

"So, what exactly do you think we are looking for out here?"

"A voice." I wasn't even sure what we were searching for, but I wanted to figure out where this feeling was coming from and what. We continue to venture further and further into the woods as I try to follow the strange feeling in my gut.

"Angel," a familiar voice calls out. I turn in the direction it came from and shield Justin with my body. Justin backs himself into my side, his eyes on the woods in front of us.

"Show yourself!" I call out as the sound of what appears to be paws fills my ears. After a few seconds, dark green eyes come into view from behind a bush, gleaming towards me. *Could she be what was calling to me in the dream?* I think to myself as quietly as possible.

"Angel, we need to talk about important matters. Now please, show me your true form so I can show you myself." She hides behind a large bush, concealing all of her dark, furry body. I slowly stand, looking back at Justin worriedly. Why would she need to see my true form, and how does she know I have one? Within a few seconds, I am my cheetah-self, ready to defend him from the new stranger.

A black panther emerges from the brush, her eyes locked on mine. She has a slim but powerful appearance. Her legs are long and muscular, moving effortlessly as she steps. Dark spots are littered throughout her body. The green in her eyes gives me a taste of hope; is there a chance she could be like me?

"I am Midnight, one of the few shapeshifters left out here. We can shift into only one animal, though, the one we chose. You are quite different. I've seen you change into many animals, and very easily too. You have so much to learn...along with your human friend." *Stalker alert. I am the only one that can shift into any animal I choose. Why is it this way? I know I have enough questions to accept her offer, but she is strange nonetheless.*

"Including how terribly you think. If you want no one to hear what you say to yourself, think of a tough barrier, like a wall as you do so. There is another way, but it's harder to learn, and you are not ready."

"Justin?" I look at him for his say in the matter.

"Well... maybe she knows things that could be useful in the future. I say we can trust her."

"Glad you are on board. Now hop on her back, and let's go." Justin and I exchange confused glances; we have never tried this sort of thing before. I crouch down as low as I can and shift my wings back somewhat as he climbs on. He positions himself right behind them, grabbing underneath and hooking his arms around for grip. Midnight takes off into a run, making me quickly follow as Justin situates himself. As my speed increases, I can feel his legs slowly shifting backward as he struggles to fight the wind.

"Heels down, toes up! And lean forward," Midnight calls from ahead. He instantly leans forward more to help fight the wind and squeezes my sides with his legs to try and stay in place.

We follow her even deeper into the forest, crossing a shallow river filled with sparkling water. The water feels cool on my paws as I stop for a second to take a refreshing drink, followed by an angry hiss from Midnight urging me to hurry up.

"It's just past these trees here," she shouts from behind the tree line. I slowly walk through some dense brush, only for the forest to open into a beautiful meadow full of colorful flowers and bright green grass. I almost miss the sight of Midnight disappearing into a small hole in the ground.

"What if it's a trap?" Justin asks, tired from the effort of hanging on.

"We've come this far," I say as I jump down into the dark cave. The floor is surprisingly warm and smooth under my paws. The area is vast. The only furniture inside is a small couch next to a bed made of flowers and leaves. A few torches are mounted to the walls, lighting the cave. Midnight is sitting on the bed, looking at my amazed face.

"You live here?" I ask her sadly. What would it be like to live under the ground and not even on a real bed...?

"Yes," she stands, coming close to us. "I've been here for a long time now. It's not much, but it's home. We have more important things to talk about, however." She beckons for Justin to sit on the couch.

"Okay, we're listening," he says rather impatiently.

"Easy human. I will start with why I'm in panther form, as you are both staring quite rudely. I cannot shift back into my normal, human self because I was in this form for far too long. I've been a panther for as long as I've lived here, which has been about ten years. So please, Angel, don't stay in that form any longer than you have to." She paws at the ground sadly. I shift back into my human self with her words and sit next to Justin. The thought of being stuck as a cheetah forever doesn't sit too well with me.

"I'm so sorry...so you say your 'human form,' were you born with angel wings too?" I ask her.

"No, my dear. You are the only one of your kind, born with wings and immense healing capabilities. The creatures that came from the devil, his demons, became too much for the shifters. You were created to make our fight finally have a chance. A true angel came down from heaven." I look over at Justin's brown eyes, and he looks at me as if her words were a joke. No way am I, 'demon,' an actual angel.

"That's not possible. I am no angel; all they do is good." I laugh at her, but the seriousness in her eyes makes me stop.

"It is. You may not be the perfect Angel, as most people expect them to be, but you indeed are one. You were made differently, an imperfect angel capable of mistakes. It's the best way for you to learn right from wrong. You are destined to do wondrous things."

She explains how she was born into a family of other shapeshifters, coming from a long line of individuals chosen by God himself. They were a secret society made to bring peace within the world. Still, the shift into modern society has diminished their numbers because they haven't been needed anymore. Midnight doesn't believe that any other shifters are left in the world at this point, which has also been something Lucifer, the devil, has noticed. People now do not believe in divine things, such as Heaven or Hell.

Lucifer has begun to recruit more and more lost souls into an army of demons in recent years. He approaches men and women at their weakest points, offering them immortality, the power to shift into a dragon, in exchange for their souls. These individuals are his minions, and their strength is similar to my own... little do they know that when they do meet their end, they will suffer in the depths of Hell.

Because of Lucifer's growing recruitments, God sent an angel down to Earth for one purpose: to kill Lucifer. My destiny, according to Midnight, is to kill him and stop his plans of taking over the human world with his servants.

"But why me? I am just a kid," I say to her once she's finished. I glance over to Justin, who seems to be in a frozen state. Her green eyes meet mine.

"A kid strong enough to kill the devil," she says rather fiercely. I swallow hard.

"What if I am not up to it?"

"You will be. For only you can do the task at hand. Now, you must understand. Everything happens for a reason; it is destiny that Justin has come into your life. He has a role to play as well."

"But he's a human. How can you train a human to kill a dragon? I can't lose him," I state, trying to meet Justin's eyes, but he seems to be in outer space.

"Before I answer you, I must know, do you trust this human with your life?" she asks seriously. I look over towards Justin with caring eyes before answering.

"Of course I do. I may have only known him for six months, but it feels like forever."

"Alright. For your answer, I will train him with this." She unlocks a hidden chest seemingly quickly with her paws and holds out a case for a sword, a massive one at that. She then holds it out towards Justin, who finally ends his daze and grabs it slowly. As he starts to unwrap it, she continues on, "the Sword of Shapeshifters; the only thing on Earth that can harm a shapeshifter easily." He uncovers the dark green handle with an enormous and shiny emerald at the end of it. The blade itself is shining silver with a shimmering green tint. I begin to shiver at the sight of it.

"This sword is an angel killer," he quietly says, setting it next to himself promptly.

"Yes. It could end any chance of defending the world from the evil shifters in the wrong hands. But since the sword didn't deny you, I know you are the right holder for it. Now you just have to learn how to use the thing," she says, moving towards the exit of the cave.

"I can't keep this. It could kill you," he tries to put it back, but I grab the handle, sending a shiver down my spine.

"You have to. Let's just see how seriously sharp this thing actually-ly is," I hand it to him, showing the palm of my hand. He hesitates but gently lays the tip of the sword down on me, instantly showing blood. I rip my hand back as quickly as I can. "Well, that will be the only time we ever try that out," I say, wrapping my hand up with a piece of my shirt and taking a few deep breaths. Who knew one blade could be mightier and more terrifying than anything I have ever experienced so far? That's saying something.

"That's going to leave a scar," Midnight says, watching me as I inspect my hand. The small cut isn't healing instantly like any other cut I have gotten. "It's extraordinary. Wounds from it would be just as if you were human." *Just as if I was a human. This sword really is powerful.*

"You will return here next week, and we will begin training. Tell no one, not yet. Just you two are to know," Midnight says, gesturing towards the exit.

"We have quite a bit of traveling, and it's getting dark," I sigh, shifting into dragon form. Justin slowly backs away, knowing what I must be thinking.

"I've been asking you to fly for a while now, but I did not say I wanted in!" Ignoring his objection, I wrap my dark blue, scaly tail around him and drop him on my back, making sure to keep him between the many spikes lining it.

"Grab on to one of the spikes and wrap your legs tight just like earlier." I crouch down as he does so and open my wings as wide as

I possibly can. The sound of Midnight jumping out of the cave ends my focus for a second, but I go right back to looking up at the sky. Justin hangs on as tightly as he can with his legs with one hand, the other being occupied by the sword. With one solid push of my legs and a mighty flap of my wings, I rise about ten feet. Justin's weight barely slows me down as I continue rising with every powerful stroke. My heart skips a bit when I look down, so my eyes focus on what is above. I continue to rise, flapping with the mighty dragon wings that feel much more powerful than my own.

"We're flying!" I shout happily as we climb far above the treetops and head towards the neighborhood. Justin doesn't seem as thrilled as I am, as I can feel his grip tightening with every foot I climb. I decided it would be nice to stop rising and lower myself for his sake. I start thinking about how much he wanted me to try flying again, wondering if he regrets telling me to try again by now.

"Thank you," his shaky voice replies once we are just above the treetops.

"I should do this more often," I state, just as I notice the house a few hundred feet away. Flying gets you to places so fast, it's truly amazing, and the wind feels great on your scales.

"The house is in view," I quickly dive down toward the large backyard and gently flap my wings, so we go down more slowly. It doesn't work as well as I had hoped, though, as I end up face planting on the ground, which sends Justin into a tumble roll down my neck and over my head. I spit out a mouthful of dirt. Maggie quickly runs out of the house, horror on her face.

"Where have you two been?" She asks, helping Justin to his feet. As he rubs off the dirt, his eyes meet mine, giving me the impression that I'm the one who gets to make an excuse.

"Justin convinced me to try flying again, and I did. We have been up there all day, I just kinda got lost in the clouds, and it took me a while to find my way back. Sorry about the grass. I need to work on my landing skills," adding a small joke to the end. I just hope my lie will satisfy her worried motherly needs.

"Next time the two of you decide to go flying, give me a heads up first." She points the finger at me and then angrily walks inside. Not wanting to speak anymore, I reach out to Justin's mind.

'Are you hurt?' He gives me a shocked stare, not expecting me to use this power on purpose.

'Just a little bruised. I'll be fine.' He answers back, opening the glass slider door and heading in. The sword was resting under a bush near the fence. It must have fallen off him when he fell. I carefully pick it up, tuck it in my shirt, making sure the case is on good and tight, and scurry up to my room. I don't feel safe with keeping it outside anyways. If this thing got into the wrong hands, who knows what could happen.

I spend the rest of the day lying on my bed and thinking of the day's events. The new stranger, Midnight, offers so much for Justin and me. But could what she is saying be all lies? I have never seen any of the evil shifters or the good ones she speaks of. The fact of all of her words being true is even worse because I have no way of knowing how to kill a creature as strong as me. How could Justin possibly kill something many times stronger than him, even with the blade? He would have to get pretty close to death itself to find out.

I soon drift off to sleep, my dreams filled with mystical dragons and swords of sharpness, one of them ending with Justin being in pain. The one that woke me was far worse, though. It ended with Justin lying on the ground, blood surrounding him and claw marks on his chest, his heart no longer beating. I stood near his body, green tears streaming down my cheetah face. However, the most haunting part of the dream was my claws being covered in his very blood.

"Justin!" I scream as I wake, sweat covering my forehead. My door swings open suddenly, and a hand touches my back.

"I'm here...it was just a dream," he tries to comfort me, but my breathing does not subside.

"But it wasn't! It felt all too real." I whisper, pulling my knees to my chest and rocking back and forth. He jerks my knees away and embraces me in a hug, rubbing my back as I cover him in wet tears.

"It was a dream, and I am still here," he says. Somehow, I accidentally showed him the horrors of my dream, which made him completely calm. "Just a dream," he repeats.

"Just a dream," I say to myself just as his mom walks in. She eyes us carefully but sits quietly as my breathing goes back to its normal pace. Justin gets up to leave, but I grab his arm and whisper, "stay." There was no way I would be able to sleep again after witnessing a terrible fear I have deep inside. Justin sits back down and pulls the covers back over me, tucking the sides around me. Maggie doesn't object when he lies on his back and slowly strokes my hair.

"Just until you fall asleep," he whispers.

Chapter Seven

Training

The next few days went by slowly as they were full of even more nightmares that had me waking up in the middle of the night, screaming. I don't understand the cause of the nightmares. I just hope they come to an end soon because I need to sleep before the training session with Midnight. I can't let anything as simple as dreams stop me from going to something as important as this. Part of me is excited for the lesson, as I could learn many new skills to help me better understand my strengths and powers. But the other part of me is afraid of what the new knowledge could do. If an evil shifter hears of my training, they may come out and attack before I become stronger and ready enough to face them.

Justin seems a lot less worried than I am, though; he says that my dreams could be just that...dreams. He doesn't see how I could ever hurt him in the future, so it would be best for us to be conscious of them without letting them fill us with worry. I hoped he was right. After all, I could never see myself hurting him, either.

"Wake up!" Justin shakes me from my sleep just as a nightmare is rolling in. "She didn't give us a time to be there, so we may as well go early." He uncovers me and tosses me a pair of shorts and a t-shirt. I let out a yawn as I stretch my arms up in the air, slowly sitting up.

"Okay. Tell your mom we are going to the forest to try some more flying." I yawn once more as I pick up my clothes and shoo him out of the room. He nods and runs down the stairs and into the kitchen, where she's cooking breakfast. As I change, I listen to their conversation to ensure he says the right things. Justin isn't the best at lying.

"Mom?" he shyly asks.

"Yeah, hinny?"

"Me and Angel were thinking of going out to the forest and trying some more flying." His voice is starting to become shaky.

"Justin, you got hurt last time. I'm not sure that's a good idea," she says, seeming annoyed.

"Yeah...but..." Justin struggles to find his words.

'Say what I say. I will stay on the ground and give her some tips while she is in the air. I wouldn't dare get back on her yet.' I call out to his mind. He slowly repeats what I told him with the same shakiness. After a few seconds, Maggie says it's alright but makes him promise not to fly with me until she feels I am ready for a passenger on my back. That was easier than I thought it would be.

Once I'm done changing, I make my way down the stairs, greet Justin, and say our goodbyes to Maggie after quickly scarfing down some food. Once we are inside the tree line a bit, I shift into my cheetah self and lower myself down for him to climb on. He lets out a loud sigh and hops on.

"I know you hate doing this, but it is the fastest way to get you back to Midnight's meadow."

"Yeah. It doesn't mean I have to like it, though!" he shouts as I take off into a run. There is no way that I am going to disappoint Midnight by showing up late to our first training session.

"You got the sword?" I ask him. He answers by showing me his open backpack with a covered blade sticking out.

"Are you sure we should do this? This could lead to some serious fighting or dangerous meetings. I don't know what I'd do if I had to face a dragon that wasn't you." Justin shakes at his own words.

Maybe he is just as nervous and worried as I am.

"No, but we have to. I can't sit around waiting for something to happen."

Midnight is already in the clearing once we arrive; surprised to see Justin managing to stay on my back still. The area is not what it was last time, though. Many tree limbs and branches are scattered through the area, creating hurdles and different paths throughout the meadow.

"I can see all of the enthusiasm in your faces," Midnight says sarcastically as Justin jumps off my back.

"How is this supposed to help?" I ask, shifting into my human form. Midnight shakes her head at me.

"You can't train like that. Turn into your true form. We are going to make this the strongest part of you. As for you, Justin, we will focus on getting your speed and strength up," she says. *Someone has this all figured out, don't ya,* I think to myself as I try to barricade my mind like she had talked about earlier. Seeing no strange or angry looks from either of them, I feel accomplished.

"Alright. What do I have to do?" I ask her, standing in front of a line drawn in red paint just before the first hurdle. Midnight smiles.

"Run through the path in front of you as fast as possible. Do not stop until you reach the end. It will help you practice quick movements and stamina. Once you reach the end, turn around and go again." I give her a slight nod and look at the path ahead of me.

A small, winding path made of sticks and full of hurdles of many different shapes and sizes lay before me. I take off into a run on my four paws, effortlessly bounding over the first hurdle. I hit a small patch of mud on the landing, making my body go into a slide around the next turn. As I regain my traction, I leap over a slightly larger hurdle, instantly followed by more.

As my mind wonders how she managed to create this overnight, I feel myself stumble, causing me to slip off course and roll into the grass. I leap to my feet and immediately continue down the course, hoping she is too busy talking with Justin to notice my slip.

By the time I reach the end of the course, my fur is sweaty, and my limbs feel a sense of tiredness I have never felt before. All of the twisting and quick direction changes had taken a toll on them. I look in the direction of Midnight for a moment as I catch my breath.

The sight of Justin sword fighting with Midnight takes me off guard. She is using her teeth to hold her sword and is fighting rather well. Our practice is paying off, and Justin seems to be doing very well against her. He bashes her with the flatter part of his wooden sword, and it makes her stumble a bit, making it easy for him to put it up to her neck.

"I see you have had practice, oh young human," she says after dropping her sword. He smiles and looks up at me, surprised to see the sweat soaking my fur. He gives me a hint to get back to running before she notices. I let out a soft sigh and take off into a run, doing the course backward.

"Thank you, Midnight. Now, what's next?" he asks rather excitedly, searching for something to look at.

"Well, I will give you some weights, and I want you to start benching with everything you've got. If you want to wield the most powerful sword in the world, you better make sure you have a mighty stroke to go with it," she replies, pointing him in the direction of a bench and a long bar covered in weights. Once he starts to walk off, she now turns her attention to me.

"As for you," she shouts as I run, "be here every weekday, and run that course twice, and every week there will be more and more add-ons to it, so you never know what to expect. Once I can happily say you have mastered that skill, we will move on to combat training, starting with you against me, then we build our way up from there."

I soon stop in front of her, panting and completely out of breath. She smiles and gestures for me to follow her. Once we are inside the cave, she turns to me again, making sure Justin is still in the backroom on the bench. Quietly, she walks over to her bed and pulls something from underneath all of the bedding. It is a shirt, a really torn-up one at that. Confused, I slowly walked over to her.

"This," she sighs as she lays the old cloth in front of me, "is very special to me and a harrowing reminder of how dangerous I am. I used to love someone, and he knew of my secret, how I could transform into this panther form, and he accepted me for who I was. He was with me throughout most of my battles. He fought alongside me with the sword in his hands. Then that..." She chokes on her words.

"That awful battle came where I was stuck in that form for too long. The last thing I remembered was him with his hand on my face, telling me it would be okay..." Tears were now coming from her eyes. "I blacked out for a very long time, and when I finally came to, he was lying there, in front of me, blood covering his shirt—this shirt--his breathing was no more and claw marks were all over his body, and blood covered my paws. I killed him. I killed my love. What you must learn from this, Angel dear is that that boy is determined to help you throughout everything you encounter. Still, at the same time, he is risking everything to do so, including his life. You must cherish every memory...every single moment you have with him because you never know when it will be his last." Tears now in my eyes, I wrap my paws around her and gently pat her back with my wings.

"I will," I finally managed to say once my crying had subsided. Once I turn my head, I notice an interested Justin staring at us, probably wondering why we were just crying.

"You will what?" he asks, slowly walking up to me as I wipe my tears away with one of my paws.

"Nothing," I reply to him, not wanting to share Midnight's story.

"I see. Well...I lifted weights until my arms nearly gave in, so I think I am good for the day," he replies, trying to get off the subject. Midnight eyes him carefully for a moment.

"You are still very weak. You will feel a difference once you are truly bonded to the sword."

"Bonded to it? How can I be bonded to a piece of metal?" he questions, taking the sword out of its sheath and examining it. She takes a few steps closer to him.

"You must take a sacred oath, pledge yourself to Angel and to the greater good of humanity. That will allow the sword to give you its true potential. But, you will not receive it fully until your first kill." Justin takes a couple steps back.

"Kill? I have to kill someone with it?"

"Not just someone, but a demon. Then its power will go onto you. But you are not ready for that yet," Midnight says to him calmly.

"I will do my best to be ready." Justin's voice shakes as he speaks. She nods in his direction before turning to me.

"Now, Angel, would you care to go up into the meadow for a while and maybe practice your flying? The oath must only be done in the presence of the one giving the commands and the one pledging them." I let my ears fall in disappointment before turning myself away and hopping out of the cave.

I make my way towards the meadow's edge, sitting in a patch of daisies. The sound of crickets chirping fills my ears as the sun begins to set. I close my eyes and meditate as I impatiently wait for them to be done.

Once the sun is completely out of the sky and the stars begin to emerge, Justin makes his way out of the cave with a rather confident look. I make my way over to him, urging that we head home before Maggie starts to worry.

We spent the next few weeks doing precisely as Midnight had said, coming to training as much as possible. I went more than Justin, as school was still going on. We did our best to keep our relationship with Midnight a secret to Maggie, but we knew that the longer time went on, the more questions she would ask.

After about three weeks of running through hurdle after hurdle, my body became stronger and more flexible. It took me much longer to grow tired and sweat to form, allowing me to run the course for much longer. Midnight continually changed the course before me, adding new twists and turns and larger jumps to the point where the course covered half of the entire meadow.

Justin also grew quite a bit; he looked like a whole new kid. His arms were swollen with new muscle growth, his jawline became sharp and smooth, and his whole appearance seemed bigger. He no longer looked like a young kid but an aspiring bodybuilder. The amount of strength the sword had given him was promising, but I was somewhat worried it wouldn't be enough. *'How was he supposed to face a dragon?'* I thought to myself one day, watching him effortlessly lift the weights.

"Focus, Angel," Midnight says to me. We were about to start our first combat lesson, cat against cat.

"I'm sorry, I just can't help but worry for him," I sigh, repositioning my stance towards her.

"Do not worry; he will only get stronger. Look how much he has grown already. He is starting to look like a young man. Now, focus!" she hisses, lunging her whole body towards me. My mind is still fuzzy. I fail to jump out of her way in time. She slams into me, pushing my body towards the ground as she pins me down. Her ears flatten as she stares at me, disappointment filling her eyes.

I let out a growl, pushing on her with all of my strength, using my wings to help roll us over to where I am now, pinning her down. I stretch my wings to the sky and smirk down at her, only for her to roll her eyes. Before I can muster a remark, I am thrown off of her and rolling in the dirt as she takes off into a run, turning herself back towards me.

You need so much more than strength, little one," she says, knocking me down just as I come to my feet again. I turn my head towards her in anger, watching as she again circles back towards me. "You will be smaller than them; take advantage of it. Learn to trust your body," she pounces for me once more, causing me to leap into the air, gaining extra height with a few flaps of my wings. "Once you do that, everything will come much more naturally. Don't force it." She comes to a halt as I land back on my feet.

"I don't know how to trust my body. I barely know how to trust these wings attached to my back," I huff.

"And that is why we will start training you in flight next month, but you need to work on your skills on the ground for now. Let's continue." She says, running at me once more. *Why did I have to bring flying into this?* I ask myself, dreading the day she makes me fly.

Chapter Eight

The Truth Comes Out

"Are the dreams stopping?" Justin asks me as I walk into my bathroom to brush my hair. I shake my head and let out a sigh. I still had the same dreams, full of death and sadness.

"They are getting less frequent, but I'm still losing a lot of sleep."

"Maybe you need to stop worrying so much. Have you talked with Midnight about it?"

"No. I'm not sure I want to," I say, ending the conversation as I walk out of the room and down the steps. He angrily follows behind me. I had hoped that they would just go away if I ignored the dreams.

His mom is sitting in the kitchen, patiently waiting for us. Something about her appearance tells me she isn't staying inside today. Justin and I exchange nervous looks as she puts a few waters into her purse.

"I want to see your flight progress, as it's been a while since I last saw you crash, and you two shouldn't be going out in those woods alone; there have been some strange sightings recently."

"What kind of sightings?" Justin asks.

She laughs before answering him, "Someone told the police it was a dragon." We exchange glances at each other before she continues. "I know. They must be crazy. Still, it is causing some trouble at work. But enough of that, I need a good distraction," she says, trying to push away the subject as she gathers her things and heads out the door.

We lag behind her some, letting her lead the way into the forest.

"Do you think Midnight knows about it?" Justin whispers.

"What I want to know is if that thing is what she's been talking about. If so, there is no way I'm ready yet... I can't be," I reply, trying to be as quiet as possible. Maggie seems far too distracted to notice our hushed voices.

"No, you're not. Neither of us is. Hopefully, it stays out of sight because how are we supposed to take on something like that?"

"I have no idea. But at some point in the future, we have to."

We reach a small clearing within about ten minutes, and his mom turns to us.

"This is good. Angel, can you shift into your dragon form for me, please?" she asks, sitting on a fallen log near us.

"I guess I can." I shyly reply, making Justin back away from me a few paces as I picture my favorite dragon form, the dark blue, scaled lizard with huge bat-like wings. Once fully shifted, I bend myself downward so Justin can easily climb up on my back.

"Don't hurt him," she commands in a fearful voice, carefully watching Justin hoist himself onto my back. He grabs my front leg and jumps up rather quickly due to the increase in muscle in his arms. Within a few seconds, he is situated how he wants to be and gives me a thumbs-up as he grabs one of the spikes on my neck for support. I glance at his mom, who nods, telling me to take off.

Hesitantly, I crouch down, spread my wings wide, and jump as high as possible with a few strong and powerful flaps. Midnight had taught me how to fly better, but this is the first time I have done so with Justin on my back in a while. It is a bit more challenging to fly with the extra weight, but it is not impossible.

I dive down towards the ground and then glide right back into the air to show off to her a bit, gaining massive height. Justin tightens his grip on me, now hugging me with his legs and arms wrapped tight. I let out a chuckle and straightened my body out so we were no longer rising.

"Thanks. You keep forgetting I don't like heights all too well."

"Ha, sorry. But you know you can trust me. I'm not going to drop you, I promise." I give him a minor scare by doing a twirl. He lets out a gasp, but it's followed by a laugh.

"Don't do crazy things like that, meanie." He gently hits my rough scales, pretending that it actually hurts me. I decide to be nice the rest of the time, slowly turning myself around and angling towards the ground. I extend my legs out and open my claws up to land as we get closer. The feeling of Justin's heart pounding lets me know he's worried that we will crash again. I have been over the landing many times now, so I remain calm as I touch the ground.

The landing is harder than usual, but I still land it on both feet, which makes everyone around me breathe a sigh of relief. I use my wings to balance my upper half as I rest on the ground for a moment. Justin leans himself back, breathing a sigh of relief.

"That went a lot better than before," I say to him after a few silent moments.

"Yeah," he sits up and slides off my back to meet his mom, patiently waiting a few feet away. I think of my normal form and quickly change into it, walking up to them before they even start talking.

"Wow, your shifting sure has sped up quite a bit," his mom says, smiling at me. "You have been practicing quite a lot, haven't you?" I nod my head at her. "But I can tell you two have been hiding something from me for a while now," her tone hardens. Justin and I exchange nervous glances. "Like how my son has suddenly become very muscular, too muscular for a boy his age, and how you two are always gone. I know you like to have fun, but this is crazy how much you've been gone. I can't believe he has managed to do as well as he did in school on top of all this. I need an explanation and a real one."

My breathing quickens as I look towards Justin, and he looks just as miserable as I am, maybe even worse. His mom now stands with her hands on her hips, giving us that 'you have three seconds before I ground the both of you' kind of look. I think for a while. I couldn't possibly tell her the truth; she'd never let us back outside again if she knew. Then again, there is no other reasonable explanation for her son's massive muscle growth.

"Umm...well, we met this..." I am cut off by an animal loudly approaching us, her green eyes focused on Justin's mom. Midnight doesn't seem all too happy either.

"Ignore whatever excuse or lie they were about to tell you, my dear." His mom freezes at the sight of a talking panther, but she's seen worse.

"Okay, perhaps you can provide an explanation for me then, Miss..."

"Just call me Midnight. I have been training these two for a very important task the past few months, and I intend to continue the training for many more. They must be prepared for the future that is coming soon,"

"Wait, I think the future is already here," I interrupted her. Her ears instantly shove back, her green eyes focused on me.

"What do you mean, Angel?" her voice stern.

"There was a dragon sighting," I state, staring now at his mom.

"Oh my, it's happening sooner than I had thought. We need to speed up the training to prepare you faster." She says worriedly, starting to pace through the grass a bit.

"Um, hello? Who gives you permission to train them? And for what exactly? I am their guardian; I won't let them get hurt for something they are too young for. You're clearly a shapeshifter. Can't you handle it yourself?" she snaps at Midnight, who turns towards us.

"Angel, Justin, go on and do some combat training. You don't need to hear the same explanation twice." Midnight shoos us away from them.

Justin looks at me for a second, and I just shrug my shoulders and start to walk towards the training area a mile or so away. He slowly follows, looking back at his angry mother every few seconds, trying her best to understand what Midnight is telling her. I really hope she doesn't keep us from all of this. Sure, I'm scared of what it could bring, but I was brought into this world for a reason and can't just let that go. I must fight as long and as hard as I can for what I believe is my destiny.

"What are we going to do?" he asks once we are far enough away so not even Midnight's ears can hear us.

"Honestly, I don't know. Just have to go with it. Prepare ourselves for what will happen," I reply quietly, worried someone is listening even though no one would be.

"Alright. Want to try some sword defending then?" he asks me before we are even in the area as he pulls the sword out from his belt strap. I take a deep gulp of air and let out a sigh.

"I have to get used to that sword, so yes."

"Okay, let's try it in your normal form first, okay?" I nod at him and ready myself for his first attack. Being so close to the sword once more makes me shiver, but I push the feeling down as best as I can.

He comes at me fast, swinging the sword towards my left side. I quickly jump towards the right, my heart racing at the threat of being struck. He is not slow to attack again, as he soon comes in from the right after I regained my balance from the first jump. Once I dodge that attack, he goes for the feet, forcing me to fly up in the air above him. On instinct, I then swoop around and dive towards him, tackling Justin to the soft ground.

"That sword really makes you edgy," Justin says after I had let him up.

"I can't explain it, but it takes so much to not want to rip it out of your hands and throw it far, far away. However, I can't do that because that is your only defense against those dark creatures and me."

"Not you; you would never hurt me. That dream you keep having is just that, a dream," he replies, almost angrily. It's so hard for me to not think it means something, a dream recurring exactly the same over and over, cannot be a coincidence.

"Fine," I say just to keep him quiet. "So, what do we do now?" Justin puts his hand under his chin as if he is deeply thinking about what we should do next.

After a long pause, I begin to expect a good answer, but he only responds by shrugging his shoulders and sitting down. That is what someone spends about five minutes thinking about? I let out a sigh and decided to join him since we couldn't think of anything better to do.

My mind soon drifts off to Midnight and Maggie. How could she be taking everything she is being told? She is always so protective of us, and knowing this, she may never let us out of her sight again. But we can't run from what we have been training to do for so long now. It would feel like wasted time and a waste of my powers. I have to do something with this potential; if I knew I had these abilities and just lived normally...it would be awful.

"Do you think she's mad?" Justin asks, turning to me. It seems as though our worries are the same.

"Yeah, but Midnight is good at making people be on her side, so maybe she won't be as mad knowing we have to do this," I reply, my mind still deep in thought.

"I just hope she doesn't make us stop. What would I do after school with all of that free time?" Justin asks worriedly, resting his face in his hands.

"Your homework," I joke with him, only making a weak smile form on his face.

"Seriously though, even if she says we can't train anymore, I still will. You with me?"

"Yes."

We waited another half an hour before heading back towards them, hoping that was long enough time to talk things out. Maggie sits there quietly, with her face firmly pressed into her hands as she pushes her hair back frustrated. Her elbows sit on her knees as she is in some weird ball. Midnight is lying next to her, whispering as quietly as she can. I clear my throat as we approach, making them look up with surprised eyes. They both come to their feet, Maggie seeming rather angry.

"You two lied to me for so long." She starts, crossing her arms. I look over to Justin, expecting him to talk, but his eyes turn guilty, and he avoids her stare. Looks like I am going to have to do all of the speaking.

"We didn't know how to tell you...so we didn't," I struggle to find the right words.

"Well, you should have. Instead, you fooled me and forced me to get told what my own son and foster child were doing by a stranger!" Midnight makes an angry face but says nothing.

"She's not a stranger," I talk back, ignoring the very evil stare I am getting. "You're right; we should have told you. We're sorry, right, Justin?" I forced him to join in on the conversation. He looks at me as if I'd done something terribly wrong to him and nods slowly.

"As for you, Mr., why did you start training with her? This is what Angel was made to do, not you. You could get really hurt, and I won't allow it," Maggie says, pointing at Justin, forcing him to look at her. But something is different, no longer guilt filling his eyes, but a fire. His fists clench up into tight balls as he opens his mouth to speak.

"It has everything to do with me. There is no way she can do this on her own. I have this," he raises the sword up so she can see it, "and it is the most powerful thing against shapeshifters. I am perfectly safe, and as its holder, I am no longer an equal to other people. I am stronger, faster, and more agile and have a more powerful mind. The first time I made contact with the sword and made the oath to the sword, I changed. It changed me, you can't tell me not to do what I am destined for, and I'm sorry, mom." I look over at him, confused as to what he really meant in that statement.

"Wait," Maggie cuts in. "An oath? When did this happen?"

"The sword will only let a certain person hold it if they are pure. The way to become the proper owner is to take a very powerful oath. This oath, 'The Oath of the Sword,' as it's rightfully called, gives the human complete control over it. Even if they are nowhere near the sword, all they have to say is a few powerful words, and it will be in their hands in a flash. And this happened the first time I met them," Midnight answers.

"But what does the oath say?" Maggie asks her.

"That, my dear, is very classified information." Maggie curses under her breath after Midnight's words.

"Why can't we know?" I ask her, my interest starting to pique. Midnight sighs, her eyes turning towards me.

"It is sacred, Angel. Only the one saying the oath must know it. The person they are saying the oath for cannot hear it. Therefore, Maggie cannot know it either. Let this be the end of it."

"Well. I am getting tired, mom. Can we just go home now, please?" Justin sighs, hoping to get away from all of this tension. She slowly nods, starting to walk ahead of us at a very fast pace. I slow my steps to make sure she is too far along to hear us.

"You can't tell me anything about it?" I ask him angrily.

"I had to. It's the only way I could become strong enough to use the sword in the first place. I am going to honor that oath and not break it. Just let that be the end of it, please. Like Midnight said." He sighs, speeding up his steps to walk with his mom and try to fix things.

As I am left to walk alone, my thoughts drift to what he could've possibly promised to do for that oath that is so important he can't even tell me about it.

None of us talk for the rest of the night, as we all have our own thoughts and are too angry to say anything. The only thing I really look forward to is a long sleep, and that Justin has school tomorrow, so I don't have to talk to him right away. Maybe he'll have enough time to think and decide to tell me whatever that oath is; I mean, what could possibly happen if I knew what it said?

Chapter Nine

Lucifer

With the fear still in the back of my mind of the "dragon" every-one had been seeing, I decided to meet Justin at school so I could walk him home. Part of me felt bad for giving him the cold shoulder last night, but I had hope that this would make it better. I'm starting to think that nothing is safe for a human anymore, so I must be around him as much as possible.

I decided it's best to go in my dog form because I'd rather not worry about hiding my wings in front of a crowd of students and parents. Before leaving the house, I say goodbye to his mom in the form of a golden retriever pup, something she simply shrugs at. I think she is starting to get used to me shifting. It is a bit breezy out-side, something I can barely feel through all of this thick fur. The grass feels soft on the pads of my feet as I jog along towards the middle school.

"Look!" Some woman looks over towards what I assume to be her husband. "That dog is waiting for her kid to get out of school. How sweet." She gently pats me on top of the head as she passes by. I wanted so badly to say he's not my kid, but I decided against it and sat patiently on the sidewalk as the buses started to drive up to the front of the school. I begin to wonder how it is possible that so many kids can go home on six buses. That quickly goes away as I notice many cars also starting to pull up and park by the school.

Everything seemed relatively normal like nothing was out of place. Part of me wondered if I was just being paranoid about something attacking him. There was no way a dragon would even go after a school, right? As if an answer to my question, it was as if everything inside of me sunk. I felt as though my breath had been sucked out of my body instantly. I was cold and terrified. My entire body began to shake, and I did not know why. But something is terribly wrong. I felt so frozen that I did not even realize the woman had approached me, trying to figure out why the random dog was cowering down in fear.

I slowly begin to get my senses back in time to hear branches cracking in the woods across from the playground. A small amount of courage fills my veins, and I can take a few steps towards the wood.

"Show yourself!" I half bark, just now remembering I am in dog form. A chuckle emerges from the thick woods, sending a cold shiver down my spine. The woman lets out a shriek from behind me. I wasn't sure if it was for me or the loud snap.

"Where is the fun in that? Wouldn't you rather give those kids watching the seconds tick by for the end of class a good show?" A deep man's voice hisses, too close for comfort. I take a few steps back, the end of class bell ringing through my ears as a giant head bursts through the shrub, sending branches and leaves flying throughout the air. A large, black dragon full of red tinted scales emerges out of the trees, flapping his huge wings to glide over the shrubbery he knocked over. He lands hard on his two back legs, balancing on the folds in his wings as he takes a couple steps and narrows his dark red eyes on me.

Trying to ignore how his red eyes seem to pierce my very soul, I take a deep breath and turn myself into a dragon, flashing my fangs at him.

'MIDNIGHT!' I scream inside my head, trying my hardest to concentrate on Midnight and reaching out to her. She would know what to do.

"Angel, no!" Justin's panicked voice calls behind me, kids and parents alike standing still, jaws dropped. Where did he come from?

"Angel," the dragon repeats, a smile emerging through his toothy mouth. "You're just a kid," he hisses, slowly beginning to circle me. It is now that I truly get a good look at him. I am not even half of his size. I thought of the biggest dragon I could. His spine is full of sharp, ragged spikes that stick up between his bat-like wings. Long, thin horns protrude from behind his ear slits on the sides of his head, surrounded by many smaller spikes sticking out of his shimmering scales. His black, thin pupils stared at me like two piercing swords.

"Do you know who I am?" He asks, slowly drawing his circle closer and closer into me.

"One of Lucifer's minions," I gulp, trying to fight the fear inside me. He smiles.

"No," he snarls, suddenly propelling his body towards mine. I try to react quickly and jump off to the side, barely being caught in my side by his teeth. I let out a shriek of pain and rolled away from his jaws, kicking my back legs as hard as possible. He takes a few steps back, curling his lips as if trying to hide a laugh.

"You have no idea how to fight; this will be too easy. Maybe he made a mistake choosing you," he hisses, coldness in his voice.

'Choosing me?' I think to myself, trying to ignore the blood dripping down my side. I lower my head, watching as he inches closer to me, step by step, with his blood-stained teeth snarling at me.

"You are a pitiful attempt at killing the devil, dear child. Your body shivers in fear." He tries to distract me as he readies his body for another strike.

"I refuse to talk to Lucifer's minion," I snap, just as he lunges forward. Expecting it, I give a hard flap of my wings and rise over him, flying just below the treetops as I glide back towards him. He makes an inaudible remark as he too takes to the sky, circling right back towards me.

'Midnight!' I try to reach out once more, panic overcoming me as I dodge one of his attempted dive-bombs.

'Angel, I can feel him. Fly high; you're a strong flier. I did not expect Lucifer to show himself so soon. I am so sorry.' Her words feel like a thousand weights on my chest, and for a split second, I can feel my body fall as my wings give out from under me. *Lucifer. This is not his minion. It is HIM.*

'I can't win this,' I say back to her, steadying my wings again. I angle myself towards the clouds, with Lucifer's presence close behind. I would rather have him up here than at a school full of terrified children.

'Fight for your life, Angel. Fight. For. Your. Life.' she replies. I can feel my connection to her fade as she blocks me out of her head.

I stop flying straight up and hover within the clouds, realizing that I lost track of him. In fact, I can barely see anything this far up. It is as if I am in a dense fog that's neverending. I listen carefully, searching for the sound of his beating wings. I don't hear flapping, only wind. *Wind!* I say to myself, just realizing that he was far above me, diving straight down towards my back. In an instant, I feel the weight of his body slamming into mine, sending us in a downhill fall of teeth and claws flailing every which way. Spinning out of control, I try to reach my neck around to grab his flesh, but he is glued to my back. His back claws sunken into me just before my tail. He viciously bites at my neck but continually misses as I continue to flap my wings and flail my body every which way as we plummet towards the ground.

Knowing that the ground is getting dangerously close, I straighten my wings out as fast as possible, flipping us over so quickly that Lucifer loses his balance for a split second. Taking advantage, I use my wings to flip myself on top of him right before we crash into the ground. Pain surging through every inch of my body, we roll and bounce in a tangled mess. I try to kick myself free of him, but he manages to keep his claws wrapped around my tail. When we finally stop, I lie on my back, my spikes digging into the ground. Lucifer's dark red eyes are staring at me from above as he digs his small claws attached to his wings into my shoulders.

"This is where it ends," he says, almost completely out of breath, his eyes staring at my neck.

"Any last words, child?"

"No," I say, barely a whisper. "I am not going to die today." I try to distract him as I slowly lift the end of my tail, raising it above his right wing. Just as he opens his jaws for the kill bite, I stab my pointed tail through his wing and drag it down as far as I can. He throws his head back and shrieks. With a hard kick of my back legs, he rolls off of me. I quickly jump up and fly, diving down straight at him, jaws open wide. I latch onto his side, shaking my head to rip off as much flesh as possible. He lets out a menacing roar of pain and kicks his feet off the ground, followed by hard flaps of his wings.

Determined to not let go, I dangle from his body as he takes flight, sinking my teeth in deep to hold on. I swing my body underneath him, kicking my legs and leaving bloody scratches all over his belly. Within seconds, he does a barrel roll to knock me off, sending me falling to the dirt. I stand back up, only to watch something astonishing. Lucifer is flying awkwardly towards the ground. A large crack appears, opening wider and wider, a red-orange glow coming from within. He disappears into it, and the ground closes back upon itself as if it never opened in the first place.

Still processing what had just happened, I looked around. Hundreds of students and parents stare at me from a distance, with their jaws dropped. Panting, I scan the crowd for Justin, but he is nowhere in sight. I spread my wings to take off when a hand touches my side.

"Angel, are you alright?" Justin asks. He came up from behind me. I turn my head to face him, trying to slow my shaken breath.

"No," I say as quietly as possible, trying not to alarm the distant bystanders anymore. A few gasps can be heard. "That was Lucifer, Justin. *The* Lucifer. He almost killed me in front of all of these people...He is the scariest thing I have ever been around." Justin meets my eyes with his.

"I know, but he didn't, did he? You scared him off. He probably won't be back for a while. You saved these people. You saved me." His words settle my breathing a little, and I notice a few people have moved in closer. "You should introduce yourself to them, then we need to leave," he says, realizing that the crowd will not move anytime soon. I take a deep breath and shift into my normal self. Blood quickly stains my shirt, and I can feel that one or two of my ribs have been broken. The pain feels just the same back in this form, and the teeth marks on my side feel smaller.

I meet the crowd with my scared, green eyes. They all seem to have the same fearful expression on their faces, but none of them say a word, and half of them don't even breathe. I take a step towards some of them and clear my throat.

"You are probably very confused and scared right now," I start, not really knowing what to say. "I just want you to know that you have absolutely nothing to fear from me. I am here to protect you. Nothing more, nothing less. I am sorry that you did not know of my existence sooner, but now you do. My name is Angel, and I can shapeshift into many different animals, one of which is the dragon you saw me be today."

"That other one--the big one--that wasn't really the devil, was it?" A small girl blurts out from behind her father's arms. My eyes meet her blue ones.

"I am afraid it was, dear, but I promise you you're safe from him. He only wants me," I say to her. A woman behind me faints. I turn to the rest of the crowd, trying to stand a little taller and ignore the shooting pains I feel. "Yes, that other dragon was Lucifer himself. Yes, the devil. Yes, from hell. But please do not panic. You are all safe from him for now. In fact, I--" I try to take a step forward but end up stumbling and nearly falling before Justin grabs my arm and pulls me back up.

"No more of this; we need to leave. You're badly injured, Angel," he whispers into my ear. "Grab onto me, and let's fly home." I know he is right, as fighting the pain and trying to walk around has led me to feel slightly lightheaded and dizzy. "She is injured, and we are leaving!" he shouts to the crowd as I wrap my arms around him and prepare to take flight.

With a couple painful flaps of my wings, we are in the sky, flying as fast as I possibly can towards home.

"Well, at least I survived," I try to be positive.

"Yeah, but now we know how easily he can hurt you," he whispers.

"That's nothing," I reply, gently landing us both on our feet as his mom comes running out the door. Looks like someone watched the news. It is not anger I see on her face but worry. She quickly reaches for my side and tugs at my shirt, saying that it needs to come off so she can look at it. I follow her inside as we go into the bathroom, and she locks the door, making sure Justin doesn't follow.

"I'm fine, really," I say as my shirt quickly comes off without my consent. Long and deep bite marks litter my side. Most of it is covered in blood, which she is already dabbing away with a damp cloth. Amazingly, the bite marks pinch themselves back together before our eyes. Within a few minutes, the bites have completely healed. The only thing remaining on my skin are bruises from being knocked around so much. Two pops can be heard as what I could only guess were my ribs fixing themselves back up. I let out a small winch at the sound.

"Wow," she whispers, putting the bloody cloth in the sink. "Does it still hurt?"

"No, but it felt really weird when it healed the rest of the way. Like someone was pinching my skin back together," I reply, putting my shirt back on. *Why does healing fast feel so weird?* I think to myself, making sure to not accidentally reach out to her mind. I have gotten surprisingly better at it now, thanks to Midnight. She has taught me so much in this little time. There was only one thing that I was sure of; no way can I hide now. It's time to come out of the dark and accept who I truly am.

Chapter Ten

Only the Beginning

She was there within the night. I was woken by a loud tap on my window, scared by a glowing pair of eyes. She nearly got her eyes clawed out before I realized it was Midnight. She wasn't too happy but ignored it because she had other things on her mind.

"You realize what you have done, right? You should not have talked to that crowd! It will make it much harder for the government to clean your mess up," she growls, a hint of compassion in her voice. Just as she finished, Justin creeps into the room. Something told me that he was starting to get far better hearing than a normal person.

"Yeah, but what else could I have done? I didn't have a choice; everyone watched me and seemed so afraid. I don't want to scare the people. They deserve the truth."

"How did you get in here?" Justin cuts in, just as Midnight was about to speak. She glares at him.

"No need to change the subject, boy. You are in just as much trouble as she is," she snaps. Justin hangs his head down in shame. "Now, Angel, you have to understand something. You are just a kid yourself! I wanted you to be more prepared for this life before exposing yourself like that. I am so proud that you survived an attack from Lucifer. Still, you have to understand something." I open my mouth in protest, but she flicks her tail over my face to make me be quiet. Midnight explains that due to our "irresponsible" and "reckless" actions, we will now be training with her every single day and that I am not to show my face at all in public. She warns that the next attack could be as soon as tomorrow, so we cannot waste any more time. The more we try to object, the angrier she becomes. We had no choice but to accept the end of our free time as we knew it.

Once Midnight leaves, Justin and I don't say much to each other. It's hard to talk when you can't get your mind off of your mistakes. Justin silently leaves my room, part of me wishing he would have stayed. It would be hard to make Midnight not be mad at us any longer, maybe even impossible.

The following day, it took everything I had to get out of bed. I am too worried to want to do anything, yet I know if I don't, the consequences will be much worse than trying. With some encouragement from Justin, I roll off the bed and head downstairs for a sweet-smelling breakfast. At least there was always something to look forward to in the morning.

"Good morning, Angel. Justin told me what happened last night. I disagree with this," Maggie says, looking at my old wound worriedly. I slap it as hard as I can, making her gasp.

"See, no pain!" I say, an evil smile forming on my lips as she scowls. "Don't worry, we are in good hands. Midnight won't let anything happen to us," I reassure her. She sighs. I know nothing we do can really help her, as she is just a worrying mom, but we still should try.

"Angel, are you sure this is what you should be doing? Training every day?" she asks, looking me up and down.

"Truthfully, I don't know. I do not want to train every day, but Midnight said I have to. You saw how badly I did in the fight with Lucifer; I barely managed. So, I think the training needs to be more," I say, fighting myself. I really do not know what to think at the moment. "And I know he only tried attacking me so young to ruin any chances I have at defeating him. So, who knows how soon he will return."

"Yes, we should be," Justin cuts in. "I, nor can you, afford to see her get that hurt again. And I have to train with her; someone needs to protect her," he says, looking at me worriedly.

"Like how I can't afford to hear the oath you took?" I ask him, raising an eyebrow. He rolls his eyes and ignores me. "Fine, we better get going anyway," I say, taking the last bite of my delicious French toast and standing up.

"When will you be back?" Maggie asks. I shrug my shoulders; Midnight never told us when we would finish our training sessions, just that they would be every day.

After arguing with Justin about why he can't tell me the oath, we finally head out for our training session. Usually, these just seemed routine, but with the amount we angered Midnight last night, I know it will be something to fear. I just hope that if we progress well enough, she will lighten up and give us breaks again. I know I would be able to handle it, but Justin's body still isn't used to the amount of power he now has, so I worry he may hurt himself.

Rather than flying, I make Justin run as fast as possible while I run alongside him in my cheetah form. Although he is very slow compared to me, I feel that he is running much faster than your average kid. The strength he has received from his bond with the sword alarms me some.

Once we reach the field, Midnight can be seen sitting upright, glaring in our direction. It appears she has been waiting for quite some time, which is the opposite of what we could use at the moment.

"I'm sorry for being late; I wanted to see how fast Justin could run," I say, slowly walking up to her. Justin lags behind, trying to catch his breath. Midnight studies him for a moment, then turns towards me.

"As much as I like the idea, it is not for you to decide how he trains. I am your trainer, remember that" she hisses, walking towards small hurdles made of wood. "These," she points her nose towards them, "are for you, Justin. I want you to practice getting speed and vaulting over objects in your path. There may be times when you will have to run on your own to keep up with Angel in battle. You will have to be just as agile as she is." Justin looks at her in disbelief.

"How will it help me in combat? It's like you're trying to teach me to run from the enemy, not fight it," he snaps, crossing his arms. She lets out a loud hiss.

"You need to understand something, BOTH of you. These creatures want to kill you and are strong. Much stronger than a human. Justin, you are human. They are beasts. They are fast and strong, without effort. They will try and take advantage of the fact that you cannot shift like they can. So, to beat them, you must take advantage of your speed and size to get underneath them. Understand?" she says, staring at him intently. He nods slowly, positioning him at the start of her course. "Good, now do as many laps as you can without getting tired. When you feel tired, push yourself until you might collapse. Then, you will be done for the day," she commands, turning her back on him and beckoning me to follow.

"You don't really want him to collapse, right?" I ask. She shakes her head.

"No, but almost. He needs to push himself if he stands any chance at fighting shifters like yourself."

"I understand that, but it seems a little h-"

"Angel. Ignore him; focus on yourself. Now, as you know, most of the shifters are dragons. This means most of your combat will be in the air. And the air is your best defense, which you learned yesterday in your fight with Lucifer. So, your first task of our training is endurance in flight. In your human form, the first step is to fly above us doing swift maneuvers, such as flips, barrel rolls, and dives. Do not land again until you feel your wings may give out on you," she says, walking over to a bed of grass and lying down. So, she will lay there while we are pushed to our limits?

Without another word, I spread my wings out and rise above the field, making Justin stop running for a second to see the commotion. It doesn't take much effort to get up here, but I have never done the moves she is asking of me. How do I even roll in the sky with these huge things? I tell myself I should start with the one that seems the easiest: diving. I have watched many birds glide down, then moments before they hit the ground miraculously, just spread their wings and gain height again. I will not dare to get close to the ground yet, however.

I climb as high as I dare, reaching just below a few drifting clouds. Justin and Midnight are now just tiny specs below me, which I can barely see despite my amazing vision. After a few deep breaths, I angle my head and shoulders down towards the ground and fold my wings closer to my body. I do not dare to breathe as my body soars downward at a terrifying pace, the wind making my eyes water. Without much thought, I open my wings back up and glide straight forward in one abrupt motion that causes me to become slightly dizzy. My body falls about twenty feet before I regain my balance, only forty feet above the field. As I hover, I begin thinking to myself, *why on earth do I have to learn this? How can I learn this when I become so dizzy after diving?*

"Well done, Angel! I figured you would have tried a flip first; those are easiest!" Midnight shouts from below me, breaking my train of thought. "Now go and do it again, this time, try not to be so tense! That's the only reason your glide made you so dizzy."

Trying to hold onto her words, I climb into the sky. I don't see how flipping in midair could be easier than this, but I can't back down from diving now, especially with Midnight watching me closely. After a few more deep breaths, I angle my body downward again. Rather than fighting the wind this time, I allow it to take control. My wings fold what seems natural with the air currents as I head towards the ground. Rather than abruptly ending the dive, I let out a long breath of air and gently angle myself horizontally. This time, I do not lurch but still get slightly dizzy from the sudden speed change. I can see how diving would allow for some quick getaways.

Midnight makes me spend the rest of the training session doing dives. Each dive becomes easier, but they take a toll on my wings. I am not used to doing this much flying, so the pain changes from an annoyance to throbbing with each flap. I don't seem to be the only one slowing down, either. As I glide down for the twentieth time, I watch Justin trip over a hurdle and lay on the ground for several seconds before getting the strength to pull himself back up. I wonder how many times he has been around the course by now. Thankfully, Midnight seems to have noticed our weakness.

"Alright, come here, you two," she says, as I try to land but fall on my face from my wings giving out. Justin tries to rush to my side but is half-running, half-limping over.

"I'm fine," I say to him as he reaches to help me up.

"Your wings look ruffled; you've never flown that much before. Are you sure you're okay?" he says, helping me to my feet.

"They'll be fine," Midnight cuts in. "Have you never seen a baby bird learning to fly? They don't look very pretty, but they are strong and beautiful once they get the hang of it." I roll my eyes.

"Are we done? Justin looks like he can't take another step," I say, looking him up and down. He shakes his head, trying to act all strong.

"Yes, I will be satisfied for today. Just ice your wings for about an hour, and they'll be as good as new. And Justin," she turns towards him, "take a hot bath to relax your muscles; it should allow your body to repair itself quicker. Although you do not heal as fast as she does, it is fast enough to where you will not be sore tomorrow."

"He heals faster now, too?" I ask.

"Yes, but not magically fast like you, dear. Just quicker than your average human. Now run along, I expect you here...EARLIER than today. Who knows how quickly they'll reopen Justin's school," she snaps, disappearing into her cave. How can she expect him to recover overnight?

"Can you walk?" I ask.

"Not really," Justin replies, looking as though he might fall over. Without hesitation, I turn myself into a large, white wolf and bend down so he can climb on me. "Is this safe?"

"You'll be fine, just hold on tight, okay?" I say to him as he grabs the scruff of my neck. I take off in a leap, making his body fall backward slightly. He quickly regains his balance in time for another jump over a fallen tree. It takes us only a few minutes to reach home, and as soon as we reach the yard, Justin falls off my back and hits the ground with a large thud.

"Are you okay?" Without speaking, he raises his fist into a 'thumbs up' and lets his arm smack back into the dirt in one motion. It seems as though this is going to be a long night.

Chapter Eleven

The Power of Flight

The next few months go by slower than a snail's pace. Every single day we have had to go out to the field, train until we collapse, and come back the next day and do it all over again. Maggie has begun to notice and hasn't been too pleased to see her son barely able to move every night. She feels that we are being overtrained, and of course, we agree. Each day has become harder and harder for us without actually having a rest longer than sleep.

The training has had some positives, however. For one, my wings have nearly doubled in size in just the first three weeks. I can now flip, dive, and barrel roll with ease. Midnight made me train in human form for the first week, but I have been in dragon form ever since then. It is harder to make quick maneuvers in this form, but not impossible. On the other hand, Justin has become nearly as fast as I am on two legs. His legs have become much more muscular and firm; it is becoming harder to recognize him every day. However, he enjoys this and keeps challenging me to races on the way to the field.

Part of me wants to stand up to Midnight, to tell her that we have had enough. Our significant improvement needs to be rewarded with something. I wouldn't mind even getting out of training an hour early. I just feel like we need at least somewhat of a break. As we reach the field, I do not hesitate to walk up to her with a fury in my eyes.

"Same thing as yesterday, but try to last a little longer," she says to us, not seeming to notice my expression. I hold my ground, waiting for her to look up at me. I clear my throat. "Yes?"

"You can't keep doing this to us. You do realize that our only rest is sleep, right?" I say, beckoning to Justin to help me out a bit.

"Yes, and you'll get much less rest in battle."

"We are kids, whether you like it or not. We come home every night to a cold dinner, barely able to move as we climb into bed, only to wake up and leave again. A kid should not have that life. And Justin still has school; I know he's falling behind," I say, sounding as tired as possible. She stares intently at me for a moment.

"Which is why I must train you twice as hard as any adult. You're weaker than the enemy. They are full-grown men, and the two of you are children," she says, eyeing me carefully. "You know, I haven't taken a proper look at you in a while. Your wings have gotten quite beautiful, Angel," she says, adding some gentleness to her tone. My anger does not change. "Those wings, you know, are your greatest weakness."

"So, everything beautiful is a weakness?" I snap. Justin puts his finger to his lips, warning me to watch it.

"It can be. But there's a serious reason why all of your training has been flight, Angel. Do you know what will happen if your wing gets sliced by dragon claws?" She raises her cat eyebrow very unnaturally.

"I can't fly for a few days, so what. I heal very fast."

"And that, dear, is where you are wrong. Your wings have been prophesied to be extremely delicate. If they are sliced, they will heal much slower. They are full of magic; if a wing were to be torn off, you would likely die." Justin swallows hard. "And a small tear? You can no longer shift. You are stuck in your true form until healed." At first, it was tough to process her words. It seems impossible to believe that even a small tear would make my shifting powers disappear. *All of my magic is in the wings?*

"So... what if I am in an animal form without wings? Am I still vulnerable?" I say quietly, trying to not sound terrified.

"Yes and no. When you shift into, let's say, a wolf, your wings fold up and go inside your body, like a turtle hiding in his shell. But, if you are injured very badly in battle, you will forcibly shift into your normal form. This leaves you weak and a very easy kill." Her words send a shiver down my spine. Slowly, I am beginning to understand why it is so important for me to gain strength in my wings.

"Now, I hope you understand just how important and valuable your wings truly are. They are your lifeline. Although a tear may ruin your shifting ability, it will be difficult to do so. Harder than slicing Lucifer's wing was, I would imagine."

"I think so," I say, stretching them out as far as they'll reach. It seems to rejuvenate my energy somehow. I bend them forward so that the tips are close to my face and begin to inspect my feathers. "They do not seem very strong, yet they can do so much. I wonder…" I trail off, taking a deep breath and concentrating my mind on them. I think of how strong the sword is, the sharpness it has. On cue, every feather on my wings hardens and takes a shimmering glass look. I fan the blade-like feathers out, feeling the new weight of my once light wings.

"I never--" Midnight gasps, eyeing them carefully. It seems I have discovered something even she did not know. "They are even more beautiful this way. Like, shining diamonds. Surely you cannot fly like this, though."

"No," I say, giving a hard shake of my wings that turns them back to their softness. "It is draining to do that with them. But, it is comforting to know I can. I wonder if there are other things I can do with them?" I ask no one in particular.

"Perhaps," Midnight starts. "There are many things about you that are still a great mystery. I truly am excited to see you grow. I think you will amaze many people throughout your life, Angel." She sounds almost proud. "Now, I know I am hard on you two. So, I will start allowing you to go two days a week without training," Justin and I both perk up. "But," she continues, "it will be important for you to remember why we are doing all of this. And just how important you two truly are." With her last words, she allows us to leave for the rest of the day. Relief washes over me. Turning my wings to weapons took up a lot of my strength, and she must have noticed. Still, I am excited to grow and see how my power changes.

When we reach the house, Maggie seems surprised but happy. It has been weeks since we have been in the house before dinner. She prepares lunch for us then wanders off to make a few phone calls. She has been on the phone a lot lately. Most nights when we got home from training, she would say hello then go back to talking with what I could only guess to be government agents.

I knew she had been doing a lot of work with them. After the fight with Lucifer at school, I made a huge mess of things, but they seemed to have covered it up nicely. She says most people believe it was a training exercise and all special effects. It was amazing how much the public could be persuaded by the government.

After lunch, I head up to my room to relax and have some peace and quiet. The bed feels soothing as I lay right on my wings. It has never been uncomfortable to lay on them; they feel like an extra layer of cushion. *How can something so soft be so deadly?* I ask myself, thinking of my wings' immense power and weight for that brief moment. It was indeed an amazing feeling, but a draining one. I do not see how I am supposed to be able to hold it for very long, though.

I spend the next couple of hours forcing my wings back into the defensive state. Each change drains my energy more and more. After a while, my wings begin to ache. It seems as though the only thing I accomplish is making myself even more tired as each hold was only a few seconds.

"I don't think I have ever seen you so tired," Justin walks into the room. I let out a disappointed huff. "You were doing that thing with them, weren't you?" I nod slowly, keeping my heavy eyes closed. "Maybe it's something you aren't supposed to be doing yet. I wouldn't go spending your off days doing that, though. We are supposed to be resting after all." I slowly sit myself up. I knew he was right, but I feel a strong need to explore them more.

"It could be. But it just makes me wonder… There are bound to be more things I can do with them, right? Midnight doesn't know everything. I mean, how can she? I am just some prophecy to her. I am sure they didn't have every detail down," I say, weakly inspecting my wings. "They're the source of everything I am. So they must have powers of their own. I am just not strong enough to use them yet. But I will be."

"I don't think she knows everything, but we are barely beginning to learn our strength as it is. I mean, look at us. We are kids, after all."

We spend the rest of the afternoon hypothesizing crazy things that we can accomplish as we grow, making up ideas on things we can try. We talk about the days to come and how uncertain and scared we are about when Lucifer will come next. All we know is that we have to be ready. Before we know it, it is dinner time.

Maggie is barely getting off the phone by the time we come down. She explains that the government has been trying to convince her to let them talk to me, but they don't have the right since I am young. The media has been all over the dragon battle, as someone posted a video of it online. They are also finally opening the school back up, although most students are online now, Justin included. She doesn't think it would be safe for him to be in public school anymore since his face was also caught on video.

Her words make me wish he would have hidden like the rest of the kids, but it is far too late to try and regret what we did that day. He is cursed with the same hidden life as I am now. Part of me wonders if that oath he took is reversible at all. After all, should I really be forcing him down the same dangerous path as me? But it seems that is not my choice anymore.

The next morning, we both slept in, a nice reward after so much training. Maggie provides us with yet another delicious breakfast before leaving us for a meeting. We spent most of our morning playing Xbox and trying to forget about our responsibilities, which was very much needed. Boredom eventually reaches us, though, and I come up with an idea.

"How about we go for a fly?" I ask Justin, taking the last bite of a peanut butter and jelly sandwich as I look out the window. The sky is a beautiful blue with many fluffy clouds throughout it.

"Do we have to?" he asks, shuddering at the thought of being up in the air for fun.

"Yes! It will be good practice for you to get used to riding on my back," I say, quickly heading towards the back door. He follows me rather slowly. I walk towards the woods, not checking to see if he is behind me. Once I reach a small clearing, I quickly turn into my dragon self. It feels so nice to shift, the energy in me increasing greatly as I give my wings a few stretches. They feel much bigger in this form but still elegant and easy to manage. Justin's warm hands grab onto my side as he hoists himself up at the base of my neck. Once he is settled and has a firm grip on one of my spikes, I spread my wings and rise to the sky in a quick motion. I can feel Justin's hands shake as we reach the clouds, soaring far above the trees.

"Trust me," I say, gathering as much speed as possible. It feels so nice to feel the wind on my scales. "This is the safest place for you to be." I stop flapping my wings and glide through the clouds, letting us drop slightly as we go. His weight on my back barely makes a difference as we continue to soar. I look down towards the treetops, seeing many fields and trees. Justin's death grip on me softens as we continue to slow to a gentle glide. He slowly raises himself up to get a better view of the world around us.

"Well, I guess this isn't so bad. It is actually kind of nice." I turn my head and give him a toothy smile.

"See, there are some good things about being able to fly. Just think, you're the only human to ever ride a dragon!" I say, letting a cloud of black smoke escape my nostrils, causing him to cough a few times.

"Oh yeah, it is just wonderful," he says, letting out a couple more coughs. I try not to laugh and angle myself back towards the house. We have managed to travel quite far already. A familiar feeling comes throughout me as we turn, sending a shiver down my spine. Justin's body tenses up. I quickly begin scanning the air below us, knowing something is not right. As I fly, the feeling of danger continues to rise.

"There," Justin says, pointing beneath us. A small, dark green dragon is flying through the sky, his head scanning the ground below. "That's not Lucifer."

"No," I reply, "but it is one of his minions. It's like he is looking for something." In that instant, another dragon swoops down on top of us, barely missing Justin as it reaches with its claws. I quickly bank towards the left and go into a barrel roll. Justin barely moves a muscle as we go, holding on for dear life.

"Hang on!" I yell to him, turning back towards our attacker. He is another green dragon, though a bit bigger than the other one.

"You were easy to find," he hisses, flying towards us again. I dive down as fast as I can. He follows closely behind, seeming to be rather determined. I bank as hard as I can to the left to get behind him. He levels his glide out and turns toward me, but as he does, my claws latch onto his neck. Determined to end this swiftly for Justin's sake, I dig them in as far as they'll go and swing us around in a few circles before releasing him. His body is sent into freefall as he flings from my clutches. I try to dive down after him, but the other dragon is already within reach. His claws grab ahold of my tail. As his body slams into mine, it sends us both into a fall. I reach my head around towards him and bite down on his throat, sinking my teeth in as we continue to plummet. He releases, wincing in pain as I violently shake my head. I swing my legs towards his body and grab ahold of his sides with my claws.

With the dragon firmly in my grasp, I dive us down towards the ground. We quickly make contact, his back hitting the dirt first and absorbing most of the deadly impact. I release my hold on him to land smoothly, but we end up rolling off of his body. I land on my side, sending Justin tumbling off my back and into the grass. I jump up as fast as possible, flying back towards the now dying demon. He lays in a bloody heap, his heart barely beating. My eyes meet his almost entirely black ones. I clamp my jaws on his neck and go in for the kill bite without hesitation.

"Angel, his friend!" Justin yells from a few feet away, pointing towards the sky. The other demon lands swiftly next to us, his eyes filled with rage.

"You were supposed to be an easy, quick kill. Now, I will make you suffer," he snarls, leaping towards Justin. I leap in front of him, engulfing him in rage fueled flames as Justin cowers behind my wing. The demon's fire reaches mine, entangling the flames as we slowly move closer together. My throat begins to ache, the fire within starting to feel like heartburn. I am not sure how much longer I can hold this. Justin shouts something to himself from the side of us now, but I cannot make it out. The sound of the flames erupting from our mouths overpowered any other noises.

I continue to step towards the demon, hoping his lungs are also dying out. My eyes begin to burn from the immense heat. All around us is a fury of smoke and orange light. With a final hiss, I am forced to take a breath and stop my flames. His fire reaches my face, forcing me to close my eyes and lower my head. The heat doesn't bother me too much, as my dragon scales are made for this. But it makes it impossible to focus on my surroundings. As I cower down lower, the flames stop instantly, and the demon's body hits the ground with a soft thud.

I open my eyes to reveal Justin with the sword driven through the dragon's neck. My eyes widened. *He did not have that with him the whole time, did he?* As Justin pulls the sword out, it lets out a soft hum, and the green shimmer within it starts to glow. I take a couple steps back, not sure what to expect.

Justin clasps it with both hands, watching as the blade hums to him and the green glow seems to come to life, coming out of the sword and swirling into the air. I hold my breath as the light seeps into Justin's nose, causing him to drop his head back and close his eyes. His body shakes with the sword as he absorbs some of its energy.

After a few moments, the humming stops, and Justin lets the sword fall from his grip as he lands on his knees, trying to catch his breath. His eyes meet mine, a faint green shimmer dancing in the brown of his eyes.

"Are you alright?" I ask him.

"More than alright, I feel so…strong. I think it gave me some of its strength. I remember Midnight saying this would happen."

"Yes, but where did you--" I ask him.

"I summoned it, and it came."

"It comes to you?"

"Midnight said, if I ever call upon the sword and truly need it, it shall come to me. And it sure did." I stared at him in disbelief before remembering what Midnight had explained to Maggie the day before Lucifer showed himself. Before I can say another word, the demon's bodies turn to black dust, creating a dark swarm that touches the dirt and seeps into it. After a few minutes, it is as if their bodies were never there.

"Kind of like what happened with Lucifer," Justin says as the last bit of the mist disappears.

"No, he was still alive, and the Earth opened up for him. This is just their death. No body, no evidence," I say, examining the spot where one of the demons was. The only thing remaining is blood-stained grass and dirt.

Justin slowly climbs upon my back, making sure to keep the sword in its sheath as he adjusts himself. I leap into the sky, feeling sore as we begin to climb in the direction of home. It is easy to remember where we are; my body just knows. Justin calls it my built-in compass.

We reached home in a couple of hours, as my soreness caused us to fly slower. We softly land in the house's backyard, the darkness of the night concealing us from human eyes. I shift back into my human form after Justin slides off. We make our way towards the backdoor, but the handle turns, and Maggie appears, Midnight by her side before we reach it. She must have seen the sword disappear.

Neither of us says a word as we walk into the house and let our bodies fall onto the couch.

"What happened?" Midnight asks.

"We flew far up in the clouds and got ambushed by two demons. They're both dead," I say quietly.

"How did they die?" Midnight continues, wanting to know the details. I explain everything to the best of my knowledge to both of them, start to finish. Maggie seems full of concern, but Midnight has a more proud look on her face, especially after knowing Justin completed his 'bond' with the sword. It seems as though we have finally done something right to her.

She explains that they will likely continue to search for us, as the ones we killed were likely scouts. And since they will not return to Lucifer, he will send more to replace them. She expects it will not take longer than a week or two.

Maggie does not seem too thrilled about this. She hates the idea of corrupt men roaming around looking for us, especially since they know our faces now. She spends an hour or so tending to Justin, complaining about how dangerous everything is as she cleans up a few cuts and scrapes on Justin that are slowly starting to heal. Seeing him in pain makes me wonder if there was more I could have done to protect him in the air battle. The worst part was probably our rough landing. For that moment, I must have forgotten I had a fragile human on my back.

Justin tells us that they really do not hurt too badly and that we couldn't have handled it better, given the circumstances. I disagree, feeling rather guilty about our rough landing. However, the one thing that we could agree on was that Midnight would need to start training us as a team. I think Justin would be safest on my back anyways, so long as we train that way and he gets used to my quick maneuvers and turns.

Chapter Twelve

Together

We spend the next few training sessions doing exactly that; flying together as a team. Midnight starts us off with me doing dives and quick turns while he is perched on my back. With each dive, his grip seems more relaxed as he begins to trust his body to know what to do.

Once we get the hang of doing dives and turns together, she spices it up by making me do a few barrel rolls and flips. The main goal is that I will do them fast enough where Justin barely has to do a thing, as my movement should keep him in place. We do the first few barrel rolls close to the ground, just in case. I lead into them with a dive to pick up speed and roll as if Justin isn't there. He squeezes me rather tight, terrified of falling off.

"You know, if you fall off, I will likely be able to catch you," I say to him as he releases his death grip from our third barrel roll.

"Not from this low," he says, eyeing the close ground.

"Most of our rolling will be much higher, don't you worry." I wink back at him. "But, I will do my best not to drop you."

"How comforting," he says in the most sarcastic tone. I respond by quickly diving the rest of the way to the ground, causing him to let out a small shriek as we softly land. I proudly walk towards Midnight, holding my head high.

"I am glad you two seem to be enjoying yourselves," she starts, not seeming too amused. "It seems like Justin is getting the hang of things. Why don't you try doing it from farther up? Do it until he relaxes more, then you can be done for the day. You need to trust her, Justin. Your life depends greatly on her, and she relies on you. You're a team. Don't forget it."

"Are you ready?" I ask Justin, who seems rather unhappy at going even higher.

"I guess so. Please go easy on me," he huffs, giving me a gentle squeeze.

With his words, I leap back into the air and take us about three hundred feet higher to start. I hover for a moment, making sure Justin can adjust himself. As he tightens his grip slightly, I fold my wings in, and we go into a short dive. After we gain enough speed, I open my wings up and send us into a roll, slightly bending them inwards to control the spin. Justin manages to hold on and lets out a deep breath as we go back into a gentle glide.

"How was that one?" I ask.

"Terrifying, but not as bad as I thought. I just have to not think about how high we are. Let's go again." He moves his hands from around one of my spikes and gently grips them around both sides of my neck. He hugs me tighter with his thighs and leans his torso far enough forward that it presses up against me.

"You just have to trust me," I say to him, trying to calm his nerves. "It is important that we get this down."

"I know, so let's not stop now," he commands, readying himself for whatever maneuver I have next.

I climb once more, making sure to go even higher this time. Justin's grip on my neck tightens as we descend into a dive once more. His body shifts slightly as we roll, but he quickly steadies himself as we level out. We continue to do it this way for a few more rolls, each time his nerves seem to steady a bit more.

Once I feel satisfied with Justin's confidence, I head back towards the ground to meet Midnight. She accepts our training, saying he has more control of his nerves, and sends us home. We had another pep talk of how important it is for us to work perfectly together in the air. We must become one, which will take a lot of patience and practice. I couldn't agree with her more, as I would hate accidentally hurting him or having him fall off. She also explains that once we get good enough together and improve our confidence, he will begin riding me with the sword in his hand. This seems incredibly terrifying, as one slip could be rather deadly for us.

Midnight believes that he will be the safest while in the air with me, but to make sure of it, the sword will have to be in hand. This will not come until we are ready, though. As she does seem to understand the mere danger of him accidentally dropping it or bumping my wings with the tip of the blade. I just hope we will have enough time to train before something like that is needed.

Chapter Thirteen

Birthday Surprise

"Okay! Flip back over, please!" Justin grunts as we fly upside down. We have been practicing this the past few days, each attempt a little longer than the last. I angle us slightly towards the ground and go into a dive, using the momentum to make us upright again. He adjusts himself as we steady, putting a hand on his stomach.

"How do you feel?" I ask him. This was the longest we have stayed upside down, lasting about ten seconds. It is hard to keep that way for so long; it feels unnatural.

"A bit queasy, but I will be alright. It is definitely not my favorite flying technique, that's for sure," he says, letting his chest rest on my neck. I slowly glide back down towards the ground, and with a few powerful strokes of my wings, we land softly in the field. Midnight slowly approaches us, a content look in her eyes.

"I would say that ten seconds is your max. It will be a useful tool but not a common one; it takes too much out of you."

"I couldn't agree more," Justin replies, sitting upright once more.

"Do you understand a bit more as to why I put you through all of that running and hurdling?" she asks him as he rubs his legs.

"I think so. I am starting to use my legs much more than the rest of me when we fly."

"As it should be. Eventually, your hands will have to be completely free in the air, so you can use the sword," Midnight says, continuing to drill us on how important our movements are in sync in the air. Although Justin should be powerful with the sword on his own, he will have a better chance at killing Lucifer's minions from my back.

"Now, go ahead and head home, you two. I hope you have something special planned for tomorrow?" Midnight asks. I tilt my head at her. "It's the twenty-sixth," She looks at me as though I forgot something.

"Twenty-sixth? Is there something going on tomorrow?" I ask her.

"Angel, your twelfth birthday. How can you forget it?" My heart drops. We have been so busy that the days blur together. I can never remember what day of the week, let alone what month. *Is it really already November?'* I ask myself.

"I don't really pay attention to dates," I say, looking towards Justin. "You're in school; how do you not remember what day it is?" I ask him.

"Online school," he says. "But I didn't know when your birthday was, so you can't blame me. We should do something to celebrate. Twelve is a great age! I mean, look at me. I am a pretty cool twelve-year-old myself." He places his hands on his hips and gloats. I roll my eyes. Sometimes his confidence in himself can be overwhelming.

"Go on now, and no showing up here tomorrow. I will see you on Monday."

After saying our goodbyes to Midnight, we head towards the house with half the day left. Maggie welcomes us happily and plans to get a cake for tomorrow and a few movies. We seldom get to spend quality time together, so she tends to take advantage of every opportunity. She also seems to have something up her sleeve, as she says there will be a nice surprise for me. I pester Justin about what it could be, but he seems to be as in the dark as I am.

While Justin works on his schoolwork and Maggie is out shopping, I lay on my comfortable bed and ponder what she could have up her sleeve. Birthdays aren't a big deal to me, as my mother usually just got us a cake for dessert and nothing more. Maggie surprised me with a new set of oversized sweaters I could fit my wings into last year. She has truly been watching out for me.

After an hour or so, Maggie pulls into the driveway. I make my way downstairs, eager to see what kind of goodies she brought. I stop dead in my tracks as Emily walks in behind her. Her eyes meet mine, tears instantly forming. I run towards her, wrapping her in my arms and folding my wings in a tight embrace.

"Hey, sissy," she whispers.

"I don't know what to say," I reply, releasing my hold on her.

"Well, we can start by saying happy early birthday." She smiles, handing me a card. "Jake signed it too, but he didn't feel right coming here." I open it slowly. *Jake wrote to me?*

"Happy birthday, sis...I miss you. Love, Jake." I read aloud, pausing at his words. "He could have come too, I don't mind."

"I think he is scared of you. Especially after watching the news, seeing you turn into a dragon and all." Her eyes brighten. "It was amazing but so terrifying. Seems like a big burden for a kid. But look at you! You used your wings." She says proudly. My mind goes back to our days of running through the forest together.

"Yes, I did. You should see me now," I reply, beckoning for her to make herself at home. I introduced her to Justin, whom she seems somewhat interested in. After all, it is not often you see a kid as strong as he is. Well, who doesn't have wings, that is. We all sat around the table and ate the pizza Maggie had brought, followed by some cake and ice cream. Once we are finished, I have Emily follow me outside to the backyard.

"Watch this," I say, stepping away from the house.

I shift into my dragon form, towering above all three of them. She steps backward, only to look at me in awe. I stretch my bat-like wings as far as they go to show her my actual size. I flaunt my size by stretching my neck far into the air and looking down at her.

"You look much bigger in person," she says, walking up to me to place a hand on my scaly neck. Warmth fills me with her touch, making me lower my head back towards her. She runs her fingers down my neck, feeling the individual scales. She traces back up towards my head, her eyes meeting mine.

"All this power…." Her hand gently touches my face, "yet, I only see you." I give her a toothy smile, then lower myself down a bit as I would for Justin to climb on my back.

"Would you like to fly with me?" I say, gesturing towards the base of my neck. Her eyes widen as she stares, debating whether or not to trust me. "The sun is about to set; it will be beautiful. And my body heat should keep you warm."

"Promise to not drop me?" she says, grabbing ahold of one of my spikes.

"Yes, Emily. I promise." I try not to laugh as she cautiously climbs up, clinging to my back as tightly as possible.

"Okay. Let's go nice and slow." With her words, I spread my wings and leap into the sky. She firmly grips me as we rise. Once we are at a nice height, I relax and begin to glide. The November air is crisp and cool on my scales. The longer we glide through the air, the more her grip lessens. After a while, she sits herself up and takes in all of the sights. The sky around us turns a brilliant orange as the sun fades away. Trees and farmlands below blend together in shades of green and brown.

"This is incredible," Emily says, leaning back and stretching her arms out into the air. "I can almost feel the clouds."

"It is truly the best feeling in the world," I reply, taking a deep breath of the thin air.

"Such a big change from the last time I saw you 'fly.' You're a natural, Angel. I knew you were meant for more. Much more." Her words send warmth through my heart.

"Thank you, Emily," I reply, gently banking us back towards

home.

"How do you know where to go? I could get lost so easily."

"Instinct. I kind of just...know. It's hard to explain."

We fly until the sun completely sets, talking about how much both of our lives have changed. She and Jake moved out of our old home because it had too many memories and into a smaller apartment in a city about an hour from where I am now. She likes it much better there; the noise helps the time go by faster. She explains that Jake is starting to mature now, but not nearly as much as I have. She is taken aback by how little I act like a child now, blaming the wings.

Once we reach home, it is pitch black outside, and everything is relatively quiet. I land softly in the backyard, lowering myself down so Emily can easily climb off. Once her feet touch the ground, I turn into my human form, leaving a smile on her face.

"There's my little sister," she says, wrapping an arm around me as we walk through the backdoor. Justin and Maggie are curled up on the sofa watching a movie. They both stand at the sight of us, trying to read our faces. I leave my sister's embrace to give Maggie a hug, thanking her for setting this up.

We spend the next few hours playing board games together, trying our best to ignore all of our responsibilities for one night. Emily and Maggie spend time talking, figuring out ways she can visit every now and then without being in harm's way. Once we realize how late it is, we send Emily on her way with high hopes that I will be able to see her again soon.

"Thank you, Maggie," I say, embracing her, being careful to not surround her with my wings.

"You are very welcome, dear. I thought it was about time for you to see your own blood for a change," she says softly, squeezing me back.

I let myself sleep in the next morning, feeling well rested. Justin greets me in bed with a tray full of waffles with whipped cream and strawberries.

"Happy birthday Angel! My mom made these for us," he says, sitting next to me as he hands me a fork. We immediately dig into the sugary deliciousness.

"What do you have in mind for today?"

"How about we be lazy and play some games? We haven't done that in ages," I say, finishing my last bite. He nods in agreement, grabbing the tray and running back downstairs. After hearing Maggie shout at him for running, he slowly makes his way back up the steps.

"We can play them in my room since it's all set up there." I follow him there, making myself comfortable on the floor in front of the TV. We spend most of the day playing games on his Xbox, still in our pajamas. It felt nice to act like a kid again.

Chapter Fourteen

It's all in your Head

"Try again," Midnight huffs, pushing at me with her mind once more. I think of the barrier again, doing my best to keep her out. Pain surges through my head as she enters, quickly hitting my pain receptors. *'Fight hard, Angel,'* she commands, seeming to have a tight grip within me. I let out a wince and thought of a wall made of iron surrounding me on all four sides. I picture its height reaching high above the trees. The pain within my head begins to subside. I make the wall thicker, imagining it to be about five feet wide, with no way in. Quietness fills me in an instant.

"Well done! I am blocked. Now, remember to try and keep this up whenever you possibly can, especially in battles. You will learn how to connect with certain people while still keeping others out."

Midnight had been focusing my training on the mind for the entire winter, determined to make sure I understood how important it was to protect myself. It takes a lot of willpower for me to concentrate enough to keep her out, and it never seems to last long enough. She explained that Lucifer has tremendous power over others and often uses it for mind control. According to her, his minions can somewhat control minds, but they are no good at it.

'You need to hold it longer,' she hisses inside my head, sending pain throughout it again. I fight back at her, pushing her out faster

than before. She gives me a proud look, only to focus her attention on Justin.

He falls to his knees, struggling to fight her off. After a few moments, he rises to his feet again, a bit of fury in his eyes.

"What did you go and do that for?" he huffs. She stands up some, raising her shoulders and appearing bigger.

"It is not just Angel that needs to learn how to protect her mind. It is important for you as well."

"He isn't like me; we have to be easier on him," I protest, glaring towards her. I didn't see any reason for her to punish him for not having the same strength.

"He is stronger than you realize, and he needs to learn. Although he won't be able to fight Lucifer off, he needs to be able to communicate with you directly, without speaking."

"How is you invading my mind supposed to help me do that?" He crosses his arms. Her ears flatten.

"You need strength. You need to be able to tell when someone is contacting your mind and feel who that person is. You need to know how to let them in or shut them out. An opponent that can get into your mind has already won," she answers, seeming rather annoyed. I relaxed, somewhat understanding where she was coming from.

Justin and I had communicated in our minds a few times before, but it was never for battle purposes. Usually, it was just when we did not want Maggie to hear what training had been like that day or silly conversations at the dinner table. Midnight insisted that if we could fully connect our minds, battles would be easier and safer for both of us.

The idea of fully connecting our minds had me wondering just how connected they would be. Would that mean he would hear my every thought? Would he be able to see my dreams about losing him? It all seemed like a foreign land.

She started us off by having me reach Justin and him trying to be able to feel me in his head before I tried anything. I would be in his mind, vaguely hearing his thoughts about trying to find the connection. *How do I even start? What is it supposed to feel like? I don't feel anything... Can she hear me?'* Many questions filled him as he struggled, looking aimlessly within himself.

I give him the faintest whisper, telling him to try and feel the warmth. A close connection feels warm, while an attack will feel cold and draining. In an instant, warmth fills my head as he reaches me.

'Found you!' he exclaims, feeling rather proud of himself. *'This feels so inviting; how do we make it last?'*

'Practice.' I say to him, giving Midnight a slight nod to let her know he was successful.

"Well done, Justin. Latch onto that feeling with her, and familiarize yourself with it. It will feel quite different if anyone else tries to read your mind. I am sure that the pain you felt with me would be much stronger. The more connected you become, the more of her power she can lend to you to strengthen your mind."

We spend the next few days connecting to one another and reaching the limits as to how far the connection can last. We started off by being in different rooms, then expanded upon that to eventually find a radius of about five miles from his end and ten from mine. If we reach out simultaneously, it can go for an even wider radius.

'Can you hear me?' I ask him from the middle of the forest. We both ran off in opposite directions, seeing how far we could get in a few minutes. I wait in silence, taking in the sun's warmth as it shines through the trees.

'Yes, where are you?' he asks, his voice sounding clear as day. I look around at the trees, full of budding flowers and dew drops. I make the image in my mind, focusing on it as much as possible. Once I have a clear picture, I send it his way.

'Wow, I can see what you see!' he says, filling me with his excitement. I hold onto it for a moment, feeling for his surroundings. The warm sun soaks into his skin, the breeze lightly hitting him. A tingle fills my hairs, making them stand on end. Something is near him, and it is not friendly.

'I'm coming to you; stay where you are,' I command him, shifting into a cheetah as I run towards the connection as fast as I can. A sense of worry fills him as he begins to sense the danger.

Within a moment, I am upon him as he stands in front of a snarling dragon, determination in its eyes. Justin wields the sword in both hands, holding his ground in front of it. I leap into the air and land beside him, letting out a growl.

"Angel to the rescue," he snaps, lunging towards us. We both jump to the sides as he goes directly between us. He gives an angry shake of his head, his eyes meeting mine. I reach into the dragon's mind, trying to read his next move. He seems to be concentrating on Justin, even though his eyes are on me.

'He's going to charge you,' I say to Justin, lowering myself down for a pounce as the dragon pretends to come after me. He leaps in my direction, only to use his wings to shift himself towards Justin. Justin slashes his side with the sword, making him fall to the ground. He clings his wings to his sides and stammers back to his feet, teeth blazing. Blood drips from his left side, staining the green grass. I stand by Justin's side, slightly in front, as I stretch my wings out protectively.

"He told me not to fight you in the air, yet I manage to get sliced by the human," he mocks, eyeing us carefully as he struggles to stand.

"You need to get that looked at if you want to live," I hiss. He chuckles.

"I cannot return a failure; he will cut me down much more painful than you would, I am sure. Do me a favor and finish the job." I look towards Justin, wondering if this is some trick.

"What is your goal?" I ask him.

"Kill the human," he says weakly. My eyes meet Justin's.

"If you don't mind…." the man says, stretching his neck out into the air." I look towards Justin.

Why would this man have us finish him?

Justin slowly steps towards the shifter, who closes his eyes gently as he raises his sword. I look away as he slices through the dragon's neck, only hearing the thud of his body on the ground.

"Every day, I get more and more reasons to dislike Lucifer," I say quietly, sitting in the soft grass. Justin steps behind me, wiping the blood off the sword.

"He is the devil, after all. He doesn't care for anyone but himself. Even his minions are nothing to him, just bodies. But they chose that life, so we can't pity them too much," he says, placing a hand on my shoulder. I knew he was right, but I wondered how many of the minions wanted to harm us. It couldn't be out of loyalty but fear.

"He's manipulative." Justin nods his head in agreement, motioning for me to get up.

"The scout could have company; let's get out of here." With his words, I lower myself down so he can climb onto my back. He quickly jumps on, his hands gripping the scruff of my neck as the sword shifts slightly in its sheath. I carry us back towards home, flying effortlessly above the trees.

"Find any trouble today?" Maggie asks as we walk through the door. She has made it a habit to check if we fought anyone, as it seems more and more common.

"Yes, just one. Lucifer is not trying very hard," I reply, sitting my human self down on the couch.

"Not yet, he isn't," she says, a hint of concern in her voice. "It's like he is preparing for something, you know? Only send a few at a time. He knows they have nothing on you anymore, so it has to be for some reason."

"Perhaps, but I think he is just trying to see our weak points. That or keeping an eye on things," I say to her, trying my best to calm her nerves. She worries about us too much in my eyes.

"Exactly. Find your weakness and exploit it. Don't you think it would be better if you stayed hidden?"

"And leave them free to attack the public? Besides, they can sense my presence as I can sense theirs. They would just come to the neighborhood and attack people's homes." She lets out a sigh and nods her head in agreement. As much as she would like to keep us locked up at home, she knows it would do more harm than good.

Chapter Fifteen
Sticks and Stones

"Judge Clearwater," Maggie says in a surprised tone as she opens the door. I sit myself up in bed. *Judge Clearwater? This can't be good...* I think to myself. I slowly get out of bed and change out of my pajamas, doing my best to listen in on their conversation.

"Hello Maggie, it is nice to see you again. I trust you know why I am here?" she asks in a severe yet polite tone.

"I am afraid not. Have we done something wrong?" Maggie replies.

"Oh no, it's not that, no need to worry, dear. I have just come to speak to Angel about some things. Is she awake yet?"

"I do not know. I can call her." I stand still, unsure if I should come before being called.

"Angel! Are you awake? There's someone here to see you!" Maggie yells from downstairs, her voice causing Justin to get out of bed in the room next door.

I quickly make my way downstairs, greeted by a pleasant smile from Leah. Her outfit is much more relaxed than in the courtroom: a plain purple t-shirt and a pair of blue jeans; her dark brown hair was no longer tied back in a tight ponytail but fell slightly past her shoulders. My eyes go to the gun strapped to her hip.

"No need to worry, Angel; I am just here to talk. Besides, we both know that we wouldn't do anything if we tried." She laughs while scanning me up and down, taking in my appearance. It has been nearly three years since we have seen each other.

"My, you are turning into a beautiful young woman. How old are you now, thirteen?" she asks. I shake my head.

"Twelve, I won't be thirteen for a while still."

"You look like you could be sixteen; it is astonishing how fast you have grown." She takes a seat on the couch, motioning for me to do the same. She asks Maggie to leave the room, and after making sure it is okay with me first, she does so.

Leah spends her time asking me how I have been and how everything has treated me here. She explains that Maggie has still been sending her reports of things going on, but she wanted to see me in person to see for herself.

"Are you going to tell me why you're really here?" I ask her, feeling fed up with all of the life questions. She raises an eyebrow at me, followed by a smirk.

"I forget how smart you are for your age. Seeing right past the small talk."

"I haven't had any time to be a kid. Matureness and responsibility are all I know," I say to her, wanting to get to the point.

"I can see that. It is kind of scary when you think of it. But, I will get to the point for you. We have been doing our very best to cover up the dragon appearances from the public, as it is something we have been doing well before you were born. But now, they are becoming more and more common. Not just around here, but everywhere. They don't seem interested in attacking the public, but that could change at any time."

"Your confrontation with one in front of the school did not help either. That one was a mess to clean up. But, the public is smart. They can tell something is going on and that it is not something the government can protect them from." Her eyes grow cold as she stares into mine.

"We are powerless against them, Angel. Our weapons do nothing. We hoped that getting some of your blood when you were younger would help, but it is impossible to analyze. The point is, we need your help. Tell us how to kill them, so we can do our best to protect the people."

"I can't because you can't kill them. They are divine creatures, Leah. I am sure you must know that by now. You have to trust me; I will protect you all to the best of my ability. If they are not attacking the public, I would call it a good sign." She lets out a sigh.

"So, you are suggesting that we do nothing?"

"Not nothing. Keep reassuring the public that everything will be fine. Maybe, if it gets too bad, you can confirm my existence, and I will help you calm them. Lucifer will not dare attack the people under mine and Justin's protection as long as I live. I will show him what Hell is really like if he does." My words seem to calm her as she lets her body relax into the couch.

Maggie comes back into the room, carrying a tray of teas. She offers us both a cup, which we accept. We all sit on the couch, talking about the days to come. Leah expects that she will eventually need to release my existence to the public, so long as I am okay with it. Maggie doesn't think this would be a good idea. We reassure her by explaining it is an eventuality, not something that is to happen right away.

After a few hours of talking, Leah is on her way once more, which sends a great deal of relief throughout Maggie. Although the visit with her was nice, it felt like we were on trial once more with some of the questions she asked us. I just blamed the judge side of her for that one. The fact that she is one of Maggie's superiors did not help us much, either.

"You would really have them share your identity?" Justin asks me as we make our way to Midnight through the woods.

"It wouldn't be putting my name and location on blast, Justin. Just sharing that the video they watched a couple years ago was real. It could give people comfort."

"Sounds more like a ploy to make it impossible for you to hide," he says, not seeming to budge.

"Don't you think people will be frightened when they learn the truth about Lucifer?"

"Of course, they will be, but that doesn't have to be your problem." I stop in my tracks, giving him a frustrated look.

"It doesn't, but it should be. We have to care about the people we are trying to protect. If not, what's the point?" I said to him, making him go quiet.

We reach Midnight in about an hour, and she is waiting near the cave entrance. I explained to her what had held us up, and everything said. She did not like that the government was even trying to fight the dragons, as it would only give them reasons to start attacking humans. She explained that this happened in the past, and what happened was a lot of human and shapeshifter deaths.

Whenever the government tries to get too involved with the workings of Lucifer, it never ends well. He does not like it when humans meddle in things they do not understand and takes his wrath out on them all. He has no mercy and will kill every man, woman, and child in his way. He is easily angered, especially when they mess up his plans. Now that I have explained enough let us see how your flying skills are doing." Midnight gets up and grabs a long stick in her jaws. She dips it in a can of red paint before leading us out of the cave. "Take this and hold it while you fly with her, do not let it touch her in the slightest bit." Justin slowly reaches for the long stick, nervousness flowing throughout him.

"I will know if you hit her with it."

I shift into my dragon form, and Justin climbs on my back, holding the stick firmly in his right hand as he mounts from the left side. It takes him a moment to situate himself with something in his hands. After a few seconds, he seems to be comfortable enough. His legs gently squeeze my neck as he holds on.

"Now, Angel. Fly as though he is not there. Do your barrel rolls and dives and a tiny bit of upside-down flying." I give her an understanding nod and leap into the air, gaining altitude as quickly as possible. Justin's grip on me tightens as we climb nearly straight up, but his body does not move an inch. Satisfied with his relative calmness, I straighten myself out before going into a nosedive. He leans forward, doing his best to stay in unison with me.

'Keep your mind open to me, and you'll be able to tell what I will do.' I break down the barrier in my mind, easily connecting to him once more. His warmth fills my head as he feels the calmness within me.

I quickly go into a roll, making us twist around several times before straightening myself out. As we exit, I take a sharp left turn and angle us back towards the meadow. I go into another dive, only to make us fly upside down for a few moments. Feeling Justin slip slightly, I twist us back upright once more. I glide through the air, giving Justin a chance to recover before going into another dive.

'You're not going to make this easy, are you?' he protests as we exit the dive, straightening out just before the ground.

'How can I? I won't be flying easily in the middle of a fight; we have to be ready for anything.' I say to him, climbing high into the sky once more.

We spend about thirty minutes in the air, twisting and turning every way we can. I did my best to make him work to keep the stick off of me, although I was sure I felt a bit of wet paint touch my side.

As soon as my feet touch the ground, Justin jumps off my back and begins to inspect. I lift my wings into the air to give him a better look as Midnight starts walking our way. Justin's hand touches my right side, just below my wing.

"I nicked you a bit; there's paint just below your wing." Disappointment fills his voice.

"Much better than I expected, though." Midnight says to him, slowly walking around me.

"Yes, but that mark could be a decent-sized slice on her side. How am I supposed to not touch her at all with the sword? Forget the demons; she should be worrying about me!" I shift into my human form.

"You will not; this is the first time we tried this, and you were almost perfect. Don't be so hard on yourself, Justin." I place a hand on his shoulder.

"She is right. And do not forget, you have two hands. You have strong legs; you surely don't need to hang on with your hands."

"It just seems impossible," he sighs.

"Have you seen yourself? Nothing is impossible. We will have to work at it. You just have to keep trying."

As the sun begins to set, we touch down for the last time, everything in my body aching at the amount of flying I have done. Justin weakly climbs off my back and thumps into the grass, letting his body lay flat. I stretch my wings out and sigh before turning into my human self and joining him in the yard. It felt peaceful to just lay there, nothing but the cool air to relax my muscles.

We lay there for a while, letting our bodies rest on the ground as the sun disappeared from the sky. I reach for Justin's hand, gently grasping it in my fingers. He takes a deep breath, closing his eyes.

"Why did we have to run into Midnight in those woods? We could be living a whole new life right now," Justin sighs.

"We would be dead without her, and so would the world."

"You think so? Would Lucifer really kill the world?"

"I know so. Maybe not kill it directly, but he would make it his. He is the devil, after all, inflicting pain and suffering to all of those who live. Imagine what he would do if no one could stop him."

"That's a world I hope we never see," Justin says, nervousness going throughout him. He knew we had a long road ahead, and we had barely begun.

Chapter Sixteen

The Road Ahead

"Are you ready?" I ask Justin. He shakes his head, slowly attaching the sword's sheath to his belt. His fingers shake as he slips the sword inside of it. I lower myself down and raise my wings, waiting patiently for him to climb on.

His left hand firmly grasps a spike on my back, allowing him to swing himself up. He easily situates himself, gripping my neck with his legs and keeping both hands firmly on either side of it. Midnight walks towards us, eyeing him carefully.

"Don't let your nerves get the best of you, Justin. If you keep that attitude up, you will certainly fail. Take some deep breaths and take it out of the sheath," she commands him.

I take a deep breath and connect myself to him, doing my best to stay calm and send the energy back to him. He inhales deeply and slowly lets the air out. He slides his right hand onto the sword's hilt and pulls it out. A tingle erupts throughout my body, feeling it close to my skin, but I do not move a muscle. He lets go of me with his left hand and uses it to steady the blade, holding it close to his body.

"Don't be so stiff, Justin. You know you won't do any killing holding it that way," Midnight says, somewhat annoyed.

"Just, give me a second, please," he huffs, taking another deep breath as he tries to relax.

"It has been a month since you have touched me with paint. I trust you fully. Now, you must trust yourself." I ease his mind. He slightly nods and shifts the sword's weight to his right hand. He gently turns it to rest diagonally across his chest, keeping it as close to his body as possible. This had been the most successful way he would hold the stick so that it would lightly tap into him rather than myself.

'Now, let me ask you again. Are you ready?'

'Yes,' he replies, leaning himself slightly forward in preparation for the takeoff. I shake out my wings before leaping into the air with one powerful jump. I angle myself so that we climb at a quick and steady pace without going too steep. Once we reach the clouds, I gently steady us into a glide, flapping my wings ever so slightly to keep us at the same height.

'Go ahead and get comfortable with it; the more loose and flexible your upper half is, the better,' I say to him as we glide through the clouds. He gently lets go of the side of my neck and places both hands on the sword, moving it from side to side as he feels how much room he has to swing. Tingles go down my spine as the sword moves close to me, my scales twitching when he gets mere inches from them. He slashes the air above my neck, sweeping back and forth at the sky. He stretches himself out, reaching my sides.

The more he moves the sword around my body, ever so close to my neck and wings, the more comfortable I become. Every swing makes me tingle less and less as my body realizes he is not a threat. I let out a deep sigh, allowing myself to relax some more.

'Want to try standing as well? You did quite well yesterday,' I ask him, remembering how he stood on my back, carefully walking down my spine as we glided through the air.

'I am not there yet; how about a dive?' he asks me, his confidence level still shaky.

With his words, I angle my head down and fold my wings in, making us plummet towards the ground at an incredible speed. Justin's body doesn't move in the slightest bit as we descend, being perfectly in unison with me.

As we get close to the ground, I level us out, ending the dive smoothly yet abruptly. We glide over the treetops, still moving at a relatively fast pace. Justin lets out a triumphant shout as we speed through the air, sending a sensation of happiness throughout both of us.

We head back towards the clouds, moving faster than the initial takeoff. Feeling more confident in Justin's abilities, I go into a quick barrel roll, flipping us around in a tight rotation. The sword comes dangerously close to the back of my neck as we do so but does not touch. I let out a sigh of relief as we level out, feeling proud of him.

'Why'd you go and do that?' he scolds me.

'Because it is probably the hardest for you to hang on to, so you can handle anything with the sword in hand if you can handle those.'

'Your confidence in me is worrying,' he replies, sliding the sword back into its sheath, safely hidden away from me.

'I need to have faith in you; otherwise, we will fall apart. Now, I think that's enough flying for today.'

'I most definitely agree.'

We slowly make our way back towards Midnight, moving through the sky and descending. Midnight was not pleased with the sight of the sword put away, but she was still rather proud that we managed to fly with it out for as long as we did. She knew it would take a while before Justin had complete confidence in himself regarding my safety. After all, it took us an entire summer for him to have the confidence to ride on me with a sword.

Minions have continually attacked us, seeming to appear about twice a month, all of which we had been able to defeat with only minor injuries. Most of the appearances had happened in the air away from any people. Still, a few had been closer to the ground where fear of being seen began to worry us.

Of course, Maggie continued to have her opinions on all of the scouts, insisting that there was a greater meaning. She convinced us to go with her on a trip, saying that we desperately needed some relaxation after all of the in-flight training we had been doing.

The car ride was relatively silent. Justin and I turned our heads out the windows, watching the scenery and wondering how much further we had to go. Maggie was sure that we would enjoy ourselves on the trip, as it wasn't often she could visit her family. She was somewhat hesitant to tell us why we had to go as well. Justin had never even met this so-called cousin before.

I could feel the nervousness throughout her as we got closer to our destination, as she tried her best to focus on the road. Her hands clenched the steering wheel as her knuckles turned white.

I shift my eyes towards the blue sky, longing to rise above the clouds and away from the stress. There was nothing better than being up there, so high up that everything seemed small. Once I reach above the first blanket of clouds, I always feel safe, knowing not a soul would be able to see me. My only worry was how brightly the sun shone on the clouds below as if it were shining over a frozen lake, reflecting all the light back on me. It was safe up there.

I feel my body shiver for a moment as I abruptly end my daydream, a black dragon catching my eyes. It is about the size of most scouts I've seen, flying far too low to the ground for comfort. He angles himself towards the busy highway we are on, and tingles shoot throughout my body. This one is different; anger and corruption consume him. He is angry at Lucifer and the world. It will cost people their lives.

"Stay calm," I command Justin and Maggie as I unbuckle myself, unlocking my door as we cruise down the highway. "I'll be back, I promise. Keep driving." Before either of them gets a word out, I open the door. Wind rushes in, making my hair fly violently around my face.

I grab the side of my door and lean on the seat, moving my legs up onto it as I prepare to jump. I push myself with my arms and legs, kicking the door shut as I fly out of the car. My body falls slightly towards the ground before a few strokes of my wings. I turn myself into a dragon, making my way towards the minion. His eyes meet mine, sending panic throughout him as he changes direction to barely evade my claws.

He banks himself back towards the highway, diving down towards the cars. I dive after him, praying I reach him in time. Squealing tires fill my ears as drivers slam their brakes behind us. I slam into his back, driving him into the cement directly below, right in front of the now stopped traffic.

I tumble in front of him a way, quickly standing myself up on my wings, letting out a snarl as he does the same. His eyes scan the cars on either side of us, the terrified people holding their shaking phones out in front of them.

"Don't you dare," I snap, reaching into his mind to see what he's planning.

A wave of anguish and violence fills me; Lucifer has betrayed him, and he wants revenge. He knows that Lucifer does not want his minions causing scenes, so this would be the best way to go against it. He is fearful of me, knowing that he will be sent back down at the end of this. His lack of hope terrifies me.

He pounces towards me with a flap of his wings as he attempts to fly over my head. I reach up with my jaws and latch onto one of his legs, sending us into another tumble of teeth and claws. We manage to separate from the entangled mass as we come to a halt on the side of the road. He immediately jumps up, focusing on the people cowering behind their cars.

A few gasps escape the crowd as I tackle him merely fifty feet from them. I bring my face inches from his and let out a snarl.

"Let this be a lesson to you," I dig my claws into his wings, slowly dragging them down as a tearing sound fills my ears. His body stiffens as he tries not to make a sound, the weight of my body holding him firmly still. "You and your friends can attack me all they like, but don't you *ever* go after the humans again. I will kill one hundred of you for every one you hurt." A few people behind the cars stand up a little straighter, focusing their eyes on me through their phones. I take a deep breath and shift my eyes to them.

"Don't be afraid; they won't hurt you anymore," I say gently. "But you," I snarl at him, "you shall be sent back to Lucifer where you belong."

"And you will die. We are coming for you, for all of you," he hisses.

I latch my jaws around his neck and bite firmly, following with a quick shake of my head. The snap makes the onlookers take a few steps back, and they watch in horror as his body turns to black smoke, fading back into the Earth.

"That video from the school was real! I knew it!" A man shouts excitedly. I stand myself up high on my wings, towering above the people that are now slowly approaching me as the sound of a helicopter fills my ears. With panic starting to overcome me, I let my mind connect to Justin's.

'We are fine. We managed to get ahead of the traffic before it stopped,' he says to me, instantly feeling my presence. *'You're on the radio; it might be best for you to come back to us now.'*

'There's a helicopter over me,' I reply, staring up at the pilot as he tries to keep it safely away from the road.

'It won't be as fast as you. Fly to me and turn into a dog when you're far enough.' I scan the crowd before launching myself into the sky as fast as possible, determined to get out of the helicopter's sight. It takes off behind me but quickly fades away as I climb into the sky. I reach the first layer of clouds in a matter of seconds.

As I go through, I think of a small bird, making my body fall slightly as my scales turn to feathers. A sense of lightness fills me as I change. I am no bigger than a hand. My sense of strength does not falter as I fold my now tiny wings to my sides for a dive.

I quickly make my way back through the cloud bank, letting Justin's connection guide me back towards them. I race over the highway, moving faster than the cars below. My eyes meet the familiar silver car, and comfort comes over me.

'Roll the window down.' I command him, slowing myself down as I fly side by side with the car. Justin's eyes meet mine with a sense

of surprise as he lowers it halfway. I dive through it and tumble onto the seat with a swift motion. I pick myself on my thin talons and let out a few happy chirps before turning back into myself.

"Angel! Do not ever scare me like that again!" Maggie exclaims, turning her back towards me in an aggressive way. "They're never going to forget you now."

"You were supposed to turn into a dog so we could pull over and pick you up!" Justin exclaims, angry eyes staring at me.

"I'm sorry I scared you, but I wouldn't change a thing. People would be dead," I say, ignoring Justin and sitting back in my seat.

"I know Angel. But you have to understand what you have done. All of the government's work to cover you up is done. The public will be terrified; they watched you kill a demon…an actual demon."

"They have to accept it. Lucifer will come here and try to take them whether they know or not, and I would rather have them know anyways. That minion told me they are coming, and we have no idea when."

Chapter Seventeen

Orion

We arrived at our destination about an hour after I flew back into the car. We pull through a big gate with "Hawk Farm" hanging over it. The entrance leads to a long gravel driveway with large green fields on either side. A few pens litter the property, all with a small number of horses in them. A small brown barn sits near an arena and round pen, about a hundred yards from a two-story house.

"You took us to a farm?" Justin questions as we pull up next to a truck. Maggie lets out a sigh.

"Yes, I took you to a farm. My cousins live here, and there's someone in particular that I want you both to meet. Can you try to be open and understanding for me? Both of you?" she asks us. The tone in her voice made me know that she needed this. For some reason, this meeting just had to go right.

"We will be, I promise. Should I hide my wings?" She gives me a relieved smile.

"No, you'll be welcomed here."

We make our way to the front door, but an elderly woman comes out before we can knock. Her eyes give me a quick scan and quickly fill with excitement. I hold my wings high and straight as we approach her.

"It's good to see you, Maggie," she says softly as she hugs her.

Justin tries to take her in. He has never met her before.

"Justin, Angel, I would like you to meet Catherine, my only remaining cousin, and a dear friend." Catherine turns towards me as I approach, reaching her hand out for a shake. I gently clasp her hand, meeting her dancing blue eyes. Her touch sends a warmth throughout me as though I have known her for some time.

"It is so nice to finally meet you, Angel. We have been waiting." Catherine places a second hand over mine with her words. "I do hope you and my adopted nephew will get along." I give her a weak smile before turning my head towards Maggie.

"Nephew?" I ask her. Catherine releases my hand and gives Justin a quick embrace.

"Let us go inside; there are lots to talk about."

We all slowly follow her inside the house, coming into a cozy living room full of soft carpet. She tells us to make ourselves at home while she goes to fetch him. I sit myself down on the couch next to Justin. Maggie sits anxiously in the recliner next to us.

"I am sorry I have kept this from you. But you need all of the help you can get." She says quietly, her eyes watching the back door.

"I am not putting anyone else's life at risk Maggie, especially your own blood," I say to her. The last thing I need is another person to worry about.

"They would be useless without the sword anyway; there's only one." Justin chimes in. Maggie gets ready to say something but is quieted by the door opening once more. Catherine walks through, followed by a tall young man. His dark black hair falls above his shoulders, curling at the ends. His hazel eyes shine like pools of honey, dancing in the sun. His skin has a slight brown tint, making him look tan. A small flutter goes through my chest as his eyes meet mine, sending my gaze to the floor.

"This is my nephew, Erin. He lost his parents when he was very young, and I have had him ever since. We are struggling some, and I hope you would be able to assist us, Angel." I look toward Catherine, a hopeful expression filling her face.

"I have so much going on… I am not sure how I would be able to…" I hesitate, not sure how to proceed with her. Erin fights the urge to meet my eyes, staring towards the carpet as he wiggles his feet.

"Erin, show her. Show them why we need her and why she needs you." I raise an eyebrow. The word 'show' could mean many different things.

"Nana, I can't just show anyone. I am meant to hide, remember?" he speaks softly, afraid to say too much. Something about the way he speaks gives me a sense of comfort.

"Look at her; do not be afraid; you are alike more than you think," Catherine says, urging him to open up.

Erin's eyes meet mine for a brief moment. I give him a small smile, not understanding what she wants of him. His eyes drift to my wings as he tries to take my appearance in. He closes them and sighs, turning himself away from us. My body tingles throughout itself as he transforms into a giant dire wolf right before our eyes. His fur is as black as night, his now hazel eyes gently shimmering with energy.

I get on my feet and take a few steps towards him, standing slightly below his eye level. His ears fold back slightly as he lowers his head, our eyes never leaving each other.

"Have you always been able to do that?" I ask him.

"For about six years now, right after I turned ten," he replies.

"I first shifted when I was ten; that was almost four years ago now," I say to him, making my way to his side. He follows me with his eyes, the worry in his mind seeming to dissipate as I shift into my cheetah form beside him. I stretch my wings as the powerful energy surge fills my veins. "Would you care to go for a run?" I ask him, gesturing towards the door with my nose.

Justin quickly gets to his feet and runs in front of us, excitedly swinging the door open. I leap out of it in one pounce, followed promptly by Erin. I stop in my tracks, looking over my shoulder towards Justin and Maggie.

'Maybe you can convince him to fight with us! Make him like you!' Justin calls me, seeming to be full of hope.

'Don't get too excited. We will see.'

Erin bounds in front of me, jumping around the grass as he waits for us to head into the forest. The amount of energy coming off of him seems to be contagious, as it sends me into a run towards the trees. Erin easily keeps up, staying close to my side as we leap through the forest, moving as fast as our legs can take us. I slow myself down slightly to let Erin take the lead, and he eagerly does so.

I keep up with him, watching his large yet graceful body easily maneuver through the trees and shrubbery. He never looks back as we twist and wind through the trees, feeling my presence closer behind. A sense of comfort fills me; *where have you been all my life?* I ask myself, watching him with awe.

We run through the forest for what seems to be an hour before stopping in a small clearing with a creek running through it. Erin takes a few deep breaths as he makes his way to the water to take a few sips. I slowly walk to his side, looking into the crystal clear water as it flows by. I lean down and drink, the water feeling cool and refreshing as it slides down my throat.

I close my eyes and take in my surroundings; it is so peaceful. The songs of birds fill my ears, singing calming songs as they go about their day. What I would give to enjoy a peaceful life.

"You don't get to relax often, do you?" he asks. I take a deep breath, letting the smell of the forest fill my nose.

"Not when the devil is lurking around every corner."

"I can only imagine; my parents were slain by his followers when I was a baby," he says coldly, taking a deep breath. My heart sinks at the thought, my mind drifting to Midnight.

"Were they shapeshifters too?"

"Yes, my father was. He turned into a basilisk. He believed that other shifters would come from the shadows and help him if he fought enough. But he was wrong," his voice gets cold. "There is no one left. Lucifer made sure of that by killing my mother too. If he knew I was alive, I am sure this would be a different story."

"I am sorry, I am not sure what to say…." I reply, trying to take it all in. It seems as though he does not shift very often, if at all.

"It is alright. I did not know them at all. We keep to ourselves here, just taking care of our animals and staying hidden. I have only met Maggie a couple times, but she has always been nice to us. She keeps my identity a secret from the government."

"I am glad you have been able to keep hidden, Erin. Lucifer is a very ruthless man. I should go as soon as possible, "I stand myself, a sense of worry overcoming me. "He always seems to find me."

"Why does he want you so badly?" he asks, a hit of concern in his voice.

"I am the only thing that stands in his way. I will kill him or die trying," I say, making my way to the edge of the clearing.

"You would lay down your life? Because of why?" He tries to understand.

"I was created to, from my understanding of it. Lucifer will kill us all."

"Because of those fancy wings on your back? It seems like a large weight on your shoulders."

"It is, but I have gotten used to it. Just do yourself a favor and stay hidden, for your grandmother's sake. He is coming, and soon. I can feel it." Erin doesn't say anything and quietly leads us back towards the house.

After another hour of moving through the woods, Erin stops just before the farmland and turns to me as I skid to a halt behind him. I tilt my head, looking towards the house now in view.

"I wish I could help you; truly, I do. Maybe someday I will. I hope you understand," he sighs. I stretch my wing out and lay it gently on his back, sending a gentle shock throughout us.

"I know. I do not expect anything from you, Erin. I am just glad that you aren't alone anymore."

"Thank you. And please, call me Orion. Erin was the name my grandmother gave me to hide."

"Well, thank you, Orion. I hope he never finds you; your secret is safe with us," I reply to him before making my way back towards the house.

Chapter Eighteen

Blood

The day after we visited Erin and Catherine was a blur. Leah appeared at our house rather unexpectedly, explaining to me the severity of everything that had happened. She thought it would be best if I did not talk to the public and let things settle down a bit first.

"I really don't think things will be settling down anytime soon," I say, sitting myself up against the couch cushions. "That minion went after humans. They have never done that before. Something is changing."

"I know, but you really freaked the public out with how you went about killing that dragon in front of everyone. They're calling you a demon as well. Have you been watching the news?" I shake my head at her. I refused to look at the TV. I knew I wouldn't like what I saw. "Well, it's probably better that way. Don't leave yourself exposed where you have cameras on you again, please. I need time to clean up this mess before you talk again."

"Got it. No talking to humans. I am sorry, Leah. Just please do not let the government get too involved. People will get hurt."

"I will do my best, but it's out of my hands. I am sticking my neck out protecting you, so just take care of yourself. I'll keep in touch." She stands herself up and heads towards the door.

"Thank you," I say gently as she leaves. I couldn't even imagine how crazy her department must be right now.

"I thought she would never leave." Justin comes down the stairs, reaching his arms out to me. I let out a sigh and accepted his embrace, laying my head on his shoulder.

"I really have made a mess of things. People think I am the bad guy now. I don't know what's worse, them thinking I am a demon or knowing that dragons exist." I close my eyes, letting my body relax into Justin's embrace.

"Probably the dragons. I would be pretty freaked out too. They'll have a new image of you once they watch you kill the devil," he replies cheerfully. I take my head off his shoulder and look him in the eyes.

"You have always had so much faith in me. Thank you."

"No need. Besides, we have a real problem at hand. We have to talk to Midnight," he jokes, giving me a gentle shove.

"I had almost forgotten," I say. I hoped we wouldn't have to talk to her about the recent encounter, but she always said to report to her. I was sure she would want to learn about Orion as well. I just hoped she wouldn't be too angry with us.

After giving Maggie a quick goodbye, we headed towards the meadow. I shift into my cheetah form and let Justin ride on my back, with the sword safely strapped to his side. We learned that it would be best to always have it close to us. We quickly reach the meadow to find Midnight sitting peacefully in the faded grass.

I slow to a walk to let Justin hop off as we approach her, trying to not be a disturbance. She sits in the center of everything as she meditates under the sun. I sit in the grass beside her without a word, tucking my wings to my sides as I let myself relax with her.

Midnight takes a deep breath and tilts her head back slightly. "We have to enjoy the sun while we can; it is quickly fading away," she says. "I am surprised it is as warm as it is; it's already November again, isn't it? It's hard for me to keep track of dates."

"Yes, it's November," Justin replies, planting himself on the other side. Midnight opens her eyes and gives him a dirty look for disturbing the peace.

"How did the trip go? Did Maggie have a nice surprise? I hope it was worth exposing yourself to everyone," she turns her head towards me. I look down at the grass for a moment, feeling the weight of her disappointment.

"It was. We met someone." I reply, trying to avoid the subject. Her interest spikes slightly.

"And who might that be?"

"His name is Erin. His father died fighting demons about fifteen years ago. You may have known him. He turned into a basilisk." Midnight's ears perk up suddenly, and she leans in close to my face.

"Benedict had a son? And his name is Erin? He told me if he ever had a son, he would name him Orion. Seems he was both a liar and an idiot," she huffs.

"He did call himself Orion but goes by Erin. He stays hidden so that Lucifer doesn't find him. Why are you calling his father an idiot?" I tilt my head at her. She softly sits herself back down, tears swelling in her eyes.

"Because I warned him that he would perish if he drew too much attention to himself. And it cost him and his wife their lives. His wife was my sister, Twilight. He had so much hope that other shifters would come to our aide. I tried to tell him they were all gone, he would not listen. And now you tell me I have a nephew who has lived in hiding his whole life."

"He is doing well, Midnight. He lives on a farm with his grandmother, and he can shift as well!" I say to her, trying to lighten her mood. Her eyes harden instead.

"If he can shift, he is only an even bigger target. It would be best if we didn't speak about him again. Lucifer is far too close now, can't you feel it? Something is happening." I nod. A sense of anxiety has begun to build up in my chest as if it were a warning.

"I can, and that dragon I fought told me they were coming for us; that definitely sounded like a warning."

"I can feel it," Justin chimes in. "It was definitely a warning Angel. They have never gone after humans before."

"I think Lucifer was testing you, wanting to see how quickly you can react," Midnight says.

"I don't know. The one on the road was full of rage. Like Lucifer had done something to wrong him. He wanted revenge," I reply to her, remembering my feelings when I connected to the demon's mind.

"Lucifer controls them, Angel. Sure, that one may have been upset. But they only do what is allowed of them. Now, I suggest that you head back home. I am not sure when the next time you will be able to see Maggie will be. Spend your birthday there, then I want you back here until Lucifer shows himself. He will come to Earth wherever you are. We need to draw him here, where you know to fight best."

"You really think he is coming that soon?" I gulp, a ping of anxiety flooding my body as my heart pounds in my chest.

"I don't know, but each day we get closer. He has waited long enough and has learned enough about you while growing his army. Do not be afraid. You and Justin are the strongest beings on this planet by yourselves. And when you are one in the sky, you are even more so. Go now, both of you. Enjoy yourselves, spend some time with Maggie. She needs you." She urges us to go, standing herself up and giving me a soft shove with her head.

Justin gently touches my side and gives me a soft pat before swinging himself onto my back. I reluctantly take off into a run back towards the house, as everything in my body told me to stay with Midnight.

Chapter Nineteen

A Cursed Life

"You can't do this to me!" Lyanna shouted to Marcus as he threw her stuff on the porch. "You're the only family I have left. Where am I supposed to go?" she asks him, tears swelling in her eyes.

"I don't care. You should have thought about it before you went sleeping around," he snaps, slamming the door in her face. The click of the lock sends her to her knees. They had been married for ten years, all of it relatively miserable. Marcus was her high school sweetheart, and she had dreamed of spending the rest of her life with him.

A crack of thunder sends a wave of pounding rain onto her, soaking her bags and body as she sits on the porch, begging him to let her in. She grew up an orphan with no relatives in reach. She only had him and tried everything to keep them together despite her boredom.

After an hour or so, she admits defeat and slowly stands her drenched self up, grabbing her bags and looking around at the gloomy world. The rain had lessened some, but the sky was still a dark grey with no hopes of clearing up. She reaches for her phone, searching for old contacts she might find, only to realize that she had blocked most of her friends.

Letting out a sigh, she slowly walks down the street, unsure where to go. She knew that Marcus would not take her back this time, as she had already cheated on him two times beforehand. He was the one who worked, so her wallet was relatively empty. *Why did I do this to myself?* She thinks to herself as a stranger catches her eye.

A tall man appears from a tree line near the road, wearing a dark cloak that flows behind him as he walks. She squints at him. It was as if the rain couldn't reach him, for he looked completely dry. She wanted to feel frightened as he walked towards her and run in the opposite direction, but something kept her in place.

"Hello, Lyanna," he says gently, his dark red eyes looking her up and down.

"Do I know you, sir?" she asks, wondering how this seemingly magic stranger knows her name.

"No, but you will. I'm here to make a deal with you," he smiles, sending a sense of calmness throughout her. Something she has not felt in a long time.

"What kind of deal?"

"The kind where you become the most powerful person imaginable. Much stronger than your lazy husband and fake friends," he says, continuing to reach into her mind to help convince her. Mortals were the easiest to get.

"I'm listening," she says quietly.

"You get to become strong and powerful in exchange for a small favor. You will be unstoppable, a valuable asset to my team. You will fly, soar in the clouds, with no humans to tell you what to do and no worldly worries."

"I'll be able to fly?" she repeats, getting excited at the thought of flight.

"Oh yes. Now, shake my hand. And you shall become powerful, and in return, I will have command over you. You will be mine but still free," he says, reaching into her mind to cloud her judgment.

Without a second thought, Lyanna's hand wraps around Lucifer's. A coldness overcomes her body as a pure black cobra appears out of his sleeve, wrapping their hands together in a tight bond before disappearing.

"One thing though," Lucifer says, as Lyanna falls to the ground, power consuming her. "If you disobey me or die, you will suffer an eternity in Hell," he grins, watching her curl up as part of his power bonds with her being. She rolls around on the ground, gritting her teeth as a cloud of black smoke creeps around her body, forming a ball of darkness. Her spine lengthens and forms a large spiked tail. Wings emerge from her sides as her body elongates. Dark purple scales cover her, glistening ever so faintly. Her eyes turn deep orange, looking almost red. Once the smoke clears, she stands before Lucifer as a dragon.

"A dragon? What is this? Some trick!" She begins to panic, walking in circles as she tries to examine herself. "You said I would be powerful! Not a damned dragon!" she hisses, anger fueling her. Lucifer lets out a chuckle.

"You are powerful, child. Now, follow me," he commands. She tries to object, but her body pulls her towards him. He raises his hand, and the Earth cracks before them. He removes his cloak to reveal large bat-like wings and jumps down into it. Lyanna stands over the edge, looking down into the abyss. A bright orange glow shimmers from the bottom, calling for her to jump into it. She hesitates, but her body forces her to leap into the crevice, closing quickly behind her.

She goes into a freefall into the depths, trying desperately to use her wings to slow her descent. She catches a glimpse of Lucifer, who is standing patiently waiting for her to land before him. With a few strong flaps, she manages to slow herself just before slamming into the rock hard ground.

"Welcome to Hell," he says, motioning for someone else to come towards Lyanna as he walks off into the distance. She shakes her body, trying to get a sense of her new surroundings. The area around her is seemingly dark, with distant orange and yellow glows lighting it slightly. She feels hot, but the heat does not bother her dragon scales.

"What is this place?" she asks the dragon standing before her.

"Exactly what Lucifer said it is," he says, motioning for her to follow. "You are now his minion, and unfortunately for us, this is our home now. We do as he says, no matter what. You signed your life away, congratulations," the stranger says flatly. She swallows hard, slowly following behind him. Walking on four dragon feet is rather awkward.

"Where are we going?" she asks.

"You ask a lot of questions. Be best if you keep your mouth shut and your head down. Do as he says, and pray Angel doesn't get the best of you." She doesn't say another word, following him deep into the depths of Hell. Many pillars of stone litter the seemingly never-ending abyss. Dragons fly around her, going every which way.

*Are these all people like me? s*he asks herself.

He takes her into a flat area, which appears to be some sort of training ground. Minions battled one another all around them, both in the air and on the ground. She felt that she could and would do better than their sloppy maneuvers. She kept wondering why they would need to be doing anything like this, though.

As she watched them, the stranger, named Jaden, began to show her the basic flying techniques. He explained the importance of us-ing the wind to your advantage to conserve energy. He said that An-gel has much more stamina than any of the other demons, so they have to take as many shortcuts as possible.

Jaden had her start by leaping into the air with her powerful legs and coordinating them with her massive wings. It was tricky to flap them at the exact moment of takeoff, but she managed to get herself off the ground after the third attempt. As she climbed into the air, she noticed a massive water-like fire in the distance, the flames dancing around each other and flowing like waves. How did she manage to get herself into this mess?

She spent the remainder of the day learning to fly alongside a small group of dragons, all of them seeming to know nothing about why they were there. Once the day ended, Jaden told the group to follow him.

He led her and the other new dragons to an entrance of a broken-down castle, where they were commanded to turn back into their human selves. Weakness overcame Lyanna's body as she shifted, the heat around her feeling much hotter. She looked at the other people around her, all of whom were older looking men with the same broken faces as her.

They followed Jaden into the castle, walking under a black arch made of two stone carved dragons, stretching their necks out, their noses barely touching at the top. *Why is it always dragons?* She asks herself as they enter a large, polished room. The floor was made of solid stone, polished so shiny you could almost see yourself in it. A large staircase led up to a throne with dragons perched on it, similar to the archway. Sitting on the throne was Lucifer himself, looking eager to see his fresh meat.

"I trust you all have decent use of your wings now," he starts, looking them over carefully. "Now, you are wondering why I have brought you here." He clasps his hands together, continuing to read them all carefully. "You have heard the name Angel," he pauses, looking through their souls. "She is a threat to my existence, and you are to lessen that threat in any way I see fit." Lyanna huffs, making his eyes instantly meet hers. "You act as though you have a choice in the matter. Do your best to keep to yourself, Lyanna. I have been sending some of my recruits to Earth, where they have spied on things for me. They are my eyes, as I can see what you see, feel, and think. Unfortunately, Angel and her pathetic human have managed to kill all of my spies. But it is no matter to me, for I will teach you all the power of mind manipulation. In roughly five days, she will be ours," he says, reaching into all of their minds at once, forcing their bodies to the ground as they squeal in agony. "I am not strong enough on my own. But with your help…." He releases his grip on them. "We will succeed."

Chapter Twenty

The Calm before the Storm

Time seemed to be moving slowly the more my body felt like something was coming. Part of me wanted to feel a sense of peace as I tried to enjoy my last day with Maggie, but I knew it was not a time for relaxation. The words of that minion still echoed in my mind, *'we are coming for you, for you all.'* Coming for us all, my mind wondered who that included. *All of humanity? My family? Justin and Maggie?*

"Angel, you're doing it again," Justin says, breaking me from my train of thought. "You're supposed to be celebrating today, not drowning in thought," he reminds me. He and Maggie continually emphasized the importance of a fourteenth birthday, but it didn't seem like anything special to me. Especially now.

"Just another year of Lucifer toying with our lives," I reply, the nervous feeling controlling my emotions.

"Don't be so grim. Let's have one day, just one," he raises one finger at me. "Of peace. No worry, no killing, no training, nothing supernatural. Enjoy ourselves like Midnight said." I raise my wings into the air, stretching out on the couch.

"Nothing supernatural?" I repeat. He shoots me a mock glare.

"You know what I mean. Let's just have a normal day." I give him a weak smile, curling myself back up on the couch. If he wants a normal day, I plan on spending it right here. There was far too much going on in my mind to move.

As if an objection to my comfortableness, Maggie walks into the room with a sparkle in her eyes. She smiles at us both, still home, relaxing on the furniture.

"There's way too much stress going on in this household." She states, pulling the blanket off of me with a quick tug. I sit myself up, arms crossed in protest. "Get up, both of you. And put this on," she commands, throwing a baggie sweater my way. "We are going out, all of us." I pull the warm wool sweater over my current shirt and tuck my wings inside with room to spare.

"Where are we going?" Justin asks, watching me adjust the sweater to fit my wings more comfortably.

"We need a Christmas tree. A real one, I am tired of our old fake one," she says, motioning for us to follow her to the door.

"Didn't we get a new one two years ago?" Justin asks.

"Yes, a new fake one. But we need to do this as a family," she sighs, her eyes meeting mine. "Because I heard you two, I know it's our last day, and who knows how long we have left." Her words send a coldness throughout me. I knew Maggie was never blind to what was happening around us, but hearing her express her fears for the coming days made it feel so much more real. I am just glad I am not the only one feeling it.

The car ride to the tree farm was relatively quiet; none of us really knew what to say to each other. It had been a while since we had done something together. The days continued to blur together as the impending battle with Lucifer seemed to inch closer. She even suggested that Justin and I go into hiding for a while to wait out whatever he may be planning. I reminded her that the world would be at risk without us holding him back. After that, she never objected to my destiny again.

The tree farm was a welcoming place. Fresh snow covered the tops of the many pine trees. The sun made their frosted tips sparkle like a thousand crystals. A few other families explored the farm, escorted by workers with axes in hand. We told ours that we would not need his help, as Justin firmly took an ax for himself. The man pointed us in the direction of the trees we would be allowed to cut without help.

Each pine tree was relatively the same size, about three more feet taller than me and a bit more than two feet taller than Justin. Sometimes I forget just how tall he really is. Maggie leads us through the trees, inspecting each one by its shape. She wanted one with full branches and a nice cone shape.

After about thirty minutes of searching, Maggie stops in front of one of the taller trees, eyeing it carefully. She runs her hand through its branches, knocking fresh snow off.

"This one," she says confidently, moving out of the way for Justin to start chopping. He readies the ax and pauses to look around for any witnesses. Seeing no one but us, he gives one strong swing and cuts the trunk clean off. Maggie claps her hands in excitement. "Nicely done! Let me help you carry it so you don't look too strong," she says, grabbing ahold of the top of the tree as he picks it up from the bottom. Once we reach the parking lot, an employee helps us strap it to the top of Maggie's car, and we are on our way.

It is nearly dark by the time we get home and have the tree set up in its base. We spend time decorating it together, spending the rest of our night laughing as we turn it into the most beautiful tree we have made yet.

The next morning, Maggie surprises us yet again. The bottom of the tree is full of neatly wrapped gifts. Justin is already sitting in the living room, eyeing them carefully. His eyes meet mine, causing him to stand up.

"Why do you think she's doing all of this?" he whispers, hoping Maggie isn't awake yet. "She knows it's only November, right?" I nod my head slowly. Of course, she does. It is so much more than that.

"She is smarter than you realize," I say quietly, stepping closer to him. "She feels it too. The stress, the quietness, the buildup." He shakes his head, trying not to believe it.

"But why have an early Christmas? We are going to be fine. We will succeed."

"I am sure we will be. Even if we win, things will be different. She's just trying to enjoy it before things change. You are the one that said normal day, right? Celebrating a holiday is a normal thing to do." He sighs just as Maggie walks into the room, a bright smile on her lips. She makes us sit on the couch as she hands us our gifts.

We both received five gifts. My favorite was another oversized sweater I could slip my wings into. Maggie knew how much I wanted to go out in public without a watchful eye on me, and this was the way to do it. No one paid any attention to bulky sweaters in Michigan winters. She gave Justin a few new Xbox games, which he seemed rather excited about.

Once we finished with our boxes, she brought out two small gifts. We both unwrap them simultaneously, revealing identical bracelets made of leather. The bracelet in my hand has a small green gem, nearly the same color as my eyes. I inspected the inside of mine and read aloud: "Light conquers all."

"In light we trust," Justin says, his eyes meeting mine.

"I thought having a little reminder on your wrist would help you work better as a team. I truly love the both of you," Maggie says, opening her arms for a hug. In unison, we get off the couch and go into her arms.

"Thank you so much, mom," I whispered, resting my head on her shoulder as I let tears fall from my cheeks. She squeezes us tighter as if she would never see us again.

We spend the rest of the day together, occasionally watching the news just in case. Not that it mattered. As of now, I could feel the presence of Lucifer's minions. But now, everything was quiet. Nothing in me gave me the warning of a disturbance, but everything inside was screaming for me to be ready. The feeling of a growing danger started out as a pit in my stomach. But as every day passed, it grew to a constant flame within me, as though my soul was giving me the biggest warning it could. I knew for sure, *Lucifer was com-*

ing. I just wish I knew when that was.

That same night, a familiar nightmare filled my dreams. I was screaming in the dark, unable to move or see. But I knew something was terribly, terribly wrong. I wasn't in control of whatever it was, and the more I tried to be, the more I panicked. It was as though I was stuck in a box with no way out and no way to see whatever was controlling it. Instantly, the box was opened, and the sight of Justin lying lifeless on the ground appeared. I jolt myself awake, covered in sweat under my thick blankets. Justin is in my room, his hand on my shoulder, trying to soothe me.

"Did I wake you?" I sigh, sitting myself up. He pulls himself on the bed, slipping under the covers next to me.

"Yes, but that's alright," he plays with my hair gently. "We've got this, okay? We have trained for years, for this moment. I don't think we could be more prepared than we are today."

"How do we know?" I ask him, then imagine his dead body stuck in my mind.

"We don't, but we have to have faith. In Midnight, each other, and God himself. He knew you could do this. Otherwise, he wouldn't have chosen you." I lean my head onto him and soak his words in as best I can. He stays in the room with me until I fall asleep, only to have more dreams that end in death. One stood out from the rest as I was surrounded by shadows. They all had different colored eyes that glowed brightly in the dark; they were black, red, blue, white, and green. One of them was trying to reach me, but I had no idea where to look.

Chapter Twenty-One

The Oath

The next morning Midnight woke me, her soft paws resting on my bed as she whispered to me. I slowly turned towards her, wondering why she would come into the house so early. I asked if she had felt me having nightmares again.

"It is time for you to come with me," she whispers, prompting me to pull myself out of bed.

"Has Lucifer come?" I ask her, my mind filling with worry.

"Not yet, but I can sense something. He is coming soon. I do not want her in harm's way." I quickly change my clothes and head downstairs, Midnight following close behind. Justin is already in the kitchen, searching the cupboards for some cereal.

"Where is she?" I ask him.

"Government business, I think. She should be back by tonight," Justin replies. My heart sinks. We wouldn't be here by then.

"Does she know we have to go?"

"She does; that's what last night was about," he answers, pouring himself a bowl.

"Well, we will see her again before we know it," I say confidently, trying to hide the shakiness in my breath. Last night may have been the last time I ever saw my real mother again. I cannot let myself fail for Justin and for Maggie. Midnight insists that I eat too, so I quickly scarf down a bowl. Before we know it, we pack our bags and get ready to head into the forest with her.

I only grab a few things, a couple of warm outfits, and some toiletries. I am back downstairs and ready to head out within about thirty minutes. Well, as ready as I can be. *This will all be over before we know it.* I tell myself, creating the steel barrier in my mind to be sure no one hears me.

We make our way towards Midnight's home, the only sounds being our footsteps crunching through the snow. It must have snowed all night; about six inches filled the ground. She walks much lighter than the both of us as I walk in my human form beside her with Justin close behind. Part of me knew that one of our trio would not step back through these trees again. I let my mind drift off as I take in the forest around me, appreciating the sparkly snow weighing down the bare tree limbs. Various animal tracks appear in the snow, going many different ways here and there.

The field is a fresh blanket of snow, almost untouched except for Midnight's faint paw prints leaving her den. Our training grounds. The place where Justin and I grew up together, fighting side by side, was about to turn into a battlefield. Midnight hoped that my presence would lure Lucifer to us.

We follow her down into her cave, which seems much homier than the first time we were here all those years ago. She had me fly her in some new furniture and beds, all of which were relatively comfortable to rest on during breaks in our training.

We both take a seat on the couch, waiting anxiously as Midnight disappears into the deeper part of the cave. She returns with something wrapped up between her jaws, carrying it as softly as possible. She gently lays it in Justin's lap, taking a couple steps back. He slowly unwraps the old cloth, revealing a shimmering bundle. He grabs it by the shoulders and reveals a complete set of the thinnest armor. It is entirely see-through, shimmering with its own light. Small linked chains make up the armor, forming a thin chainmail appearance almost impossible to see.

"It's light and delicate. But completely fireproof. It is made of the same material as the sword; it will protect you from being scratched by dragon claws. Their teeth can still penetrate you, though."

"Same material as the sword. Will it hurt Angel?" he asks, ready to drop the armor back onto the cloth.

"No. The sword is magical. It is more than just the metal in the sword that hurts her. This armor is paired with the sword, so the only one that can wear it is you, Justin. There will likely be a lot of dragon fire raining down on us, so you should be as protected as possible," she says calmly.

"It is paired with the sword? What pairs them?" I ask her, feeling more out of the loop than before.

"They were made together, crafted by God himself. He made it so the only person able to use it was the one bonded with the sword through the oath, which Justin made long ago." He slowly slips the chest piece over his head, and it perfectly conforms to his body. The rest of the set does the same. A faint shimmer covers Justin's body, flowing on the armor covering him from head to toe. It would be nearly impossible to see if you did not know he was wearing it.

"That's incredible," I say, admiring how well it suits him. The idea of having more protection on Justin soothed my anxiety some. "How does it feel?"

"Really light, I can barely notice it. I feel stronger with it too." He says confidently, swinging his arms and legs around a bit.

Midnight jumps onto the couch, sitting to face us. We both take seats across from her, knowing we are about to get some type of lecture or pep talk. She explains that she has a good feeling that Lucifer will show himself tomorrow, as she isn't sure how much stronger the feeling in her can get. I wanted to disagree with her, hoping we had more time. But part of me knew she was right. It was as though my soul was telling me so.

"There are going to be many shifters with him. Most of the time, the ones you have been fighting were likely just scouts. They won't be nearly as strong or as fast as us, but they have the numbers. We need a strategy. So, I don't want you to worry about me at all. We can use the snow to our advantage. Whenever they come, and I tell you to, fly out and fill the area with as much fire as possible. It will simmer in the snow and make everything misty."

"But won't y--" I try to speak.

"I will be fine. Fire won't hurt me. Once you have done that, take advantage of any stragglers you see struggling to fly through the haze. Don't be afraid to drop them. Go for the wings and send as many my way as you can. Justin," her eyes turn towards him, "you hang on tight to her. She shouldn't have to fly differently with you on her back. You are her protector. If she gets two or more tangled on her, or has trouble with any of them, use those muscles of yours and cut them down."

Midnight continues the day, giving us as many scenarios and strategies as she can, filling our heads with ideas for many different situations. She explains that Lucifer is not just going to be out in the open, and I will have to get through a lot of collateral damage to get him. I have to prepare for the unexpected, as he is very cunning and will be able to determine how I will strike. She reminds us how to protect our minds, as he can be rather convincing once he gets ahold of you. My body shivers at the idea.

"How come the other shifters aren't here to help us?" I ask her, remembering how she spoke of more. She lets out a deep sigh, pain in her eyes.

"I don't think there are any left. It's rather hard to fight dragons when you don't have wings," she says softly. "There used to be quite a few of us. This field was where I trained some young ones many years ago. But it seems that Lucifer either killed them all or scared them so much that they never shifted again."

"I wish I could have met more of them," I whisper, imagining what that must have been like. Orion fills my mind; *at least I got to meet him.* I think to myself, thankful he was still safely hidden.

"Well, they'd be a bit older than you are now, that's for sure," she smiles.

"Are there no more being created?" I ask her, wondering why I would be the only one created this way.

"Normal shifters are not created. They are born; it's in their DNA." Her words make the puzzle pieces in my head align, realizing why they aren't around anymore. Erin might be the last one alive besides Midnight.

"We wouldn't need them anyway," Justin pipes in, trying to lighten the mood. "We are unstoppable." Midnight smiles, nodding her head in agreement. She stretches out her paws, letting out a huge yawn, showing her pointed teeth. Part of me worried for her, but I knew she was much stronger than she looked.

"Get some rest, both of you. You are going to need it." She commands, disappearing once more to the deep part of the cave. Without a word, I lay on the couch, pulling Justin down beside me. I lay my head on his chest and cover him with a wing to keep him warm. He rests his head on mine, making himself comfortable under the makeshift blanket. His heartbeat fills my ears, soothing my anxiety as I drift off to sleep.

Chapter Twenty-Two

'Till Death do us Part

The morning is cool and humid, a dense fog moving onto the meadow. A certain aroma was in the air, a constant scent of ash filling my nose. The birds are silent, and no squirrels or critters can be found. The wind seems nonexistent as everything outside remains quiet and still. I take a deep breath, grabbing Justin's hand as we take our first steps outside. The faint clinking of the sword on his hip fills our ears as we walk out of the cave. Midnight is standing just outside the entrance, her eyes closed as she smells the air. Her black, shiny fur stands straight up along her back as she senses the imminent danger.

"It is time," she says quietly, her green eyes staring intently at the snow-covered field. Coldness overcomes me, and I let out a shiver as every hair on my body stands on end. *'He is coming,'* I say to them, taking a deep breath to calm myself.

"I love you both. I just want you to know that" Midnight voices, looking back at us with caring eyes.

"We know. We will have plenty of time after to tell each other that, Midnight. Do not worry," Justin says, pulling the sword from its sheath. As he does so, my body transforms itself into its blue dragon form, towering above Justin and Midnight. I stretch my wings widely and open my jaws before lowering down for Justin to climb on. He quickly positions himself, being careful to keep the sword from touching me.

'You're my best friend. Let's try and keep it that way for a long time, okay?' I say to him, as the Earth before us begins to split open, a loud cracking sound echoing down into the abyss, revealing a tremendous glowing light.

'I will forever be by your side, Angel,' he replies, gently running his free hand down my scales.

"God is with us," I say to them, taking a deep breath.

The crack in the Earth widens, as it had the day he first left. An orange glow emits from the crevice as the smell of ash and smoke becomes stronger. A tall man carried by two large, bat-like wings flies up, a devilish grin on his face. His dark red eyes stared into mine, sending a shiver down my spine. They glance towards Justin perched on my back, then to Midnight as she flattens her ears and lets out a snarl. His wings resemble my own dragon wings, each of the three bones ending with sharp spikes at the ends, along with two larger curved spikes where the bones come together. As he hovers above the ground, he extends his hands out to both sides, and with a quick motion, many people come from the tree line. Men and women walk out from behind the trees, all of them of many different shapes and sizes. On cue, they are transformed into their dragon forms as they spread out behind Lucifer. Even with the fog, they are relatively easy to see.

I lower myself down, not letting my eyes leave his. My jaws open slightly as I flash my fangs at him, letting out the loudest hiss I can muster. *I am not that scared little girl anymore.* I think to myself, eyeing him carefully. Lucifer smirks and motions his minions forward. Instantly, hundreds of dragons run, fly, and screech towards the three of us. I stay still, waiting for Midnight's command.

"Now," she says as they are about ten seconds away. Without a second thought, I pounce into the air and circle the area around Midnight. I feel deep within my chest and let the fires erupt out, spraying the ground in front of us. I fly as fast as possible, allowing the fires to surround the field. The flames quickly die out in the snow but leave us in a misty, smoke-filled haze as Midnight predicted.

I connect myself to Midnight's mind, constantly hearing her thoughts as she runs through the smoke. It is her best chance at fighting the demons herself.

A fury of dragons move throughout it, the sounds of their wings going every which way around us. I point us towards the sky and fly straight up, trying to get above it. The faster I get to Lucifer and end this, the better. A dark green dragon flies towards us, his claws open wide. I fly towards him, preparing for a dive.

'I am going for a dive. Can you reach his neck if I get close enough?' I ask Justin, seconds from colliding with him.

'Get me as close as you can.' He replies, tightening his grip with his thighs. Just as the demon's claws grab at my chest, I fold my wings in, sending us into a steep dive, leaving Justin free to extend his sword, plunging it into its neck, slashing down to its chest as we continue to move towards the ground.

'One down,' he says, wiping the blade.

'One hundred to go,' I reply, extending my wings to slow our dive. I meet another dragon, lost in the haze. Surprising them, I manage to sink my jaws into their neck before they realize what hit them. As the taste of blood fills my mouth, I fling my body to the side and release my jaws, sending them plummeting to the ground. As they gasp for air and try to fly back up, Midnight sinks her teeth into them and rips the throat open. She doesn't waste a second, running off towards another that didn't realize how close the ground was.

As we continue to fly through the mass of dragons, I realize how weak their flying is. Quite a few of them have collided with another and the ground. Taking advantage, I grab the attention of four seemingly lost people by grabbing one of them by the tail and flinging it into the other three.

"You'll pay for that!" he shrieks, regaining her balance in the air.

Her shimmering purple scales stood out in the fog. I turn myself around, diving straight towards the ground. They all follow, trying their best to copy the dive. I open my wings before the ground, abruptly ending it and gliding feet above the ground. I bank towards the left, turning just in time to see two of the four land hard, sending an explosion of snow into the air as they tumble. Midnight is on the scene, immediately jumping on one of their backs. She claws at their right wing, tearing the thin membrane. I clasp my claws around its neck, forcing its head into the ground as Midnight leaps at the other dragon.

The third dragon comes from above us, diving towards Justin. He stands up, balancing on my neck as he readies himself for her. She extends her claws towards him, preparing to land on us with as much force as possible. As she hits us, he stabs the sword into her chest. We fall to the ground, throwing her body to the side as I roll off the other dragon.

"Are you alright?" Midnight runs to us, the fur around her mouth stained with blood.

"Yes, we are okay," I say, staying still as Justin climbs back onto me. "Stay safe, Midnight." I fly away from her, not wanting to draw them all to one place as the smoke slowly clears. We cut down as many dragons as possible, determined to send as many to the ground as possible. I slam into as many as I can, giving Justin enough time to slice into them one at a time.

I let my mind wander for a moment, letting Justin's skill give me a sense of comfort. *The sword indeed did bless him with great strength.* Another minion slamming into my side puts me in a daze for a moment, making us fall several feet.

'Focus Angel, there are many more,' Justin encourages me, giving my scales a gentle pat as I shake the dizziness off.

'Sorry, I just can't help but notice how much you have grown. ' I reply to him, ' let's go back up, feeling like a proud sister.

As we fly up, a dark blue dragon flies directly towards us. I dive straight down, angling myself so that we go directly below them.

We go into a flip, flying upside down above their back, just close enough for Justin to slash its wings. Its body quickly plummets to the ground. I flip us back around, only to slam into yet another dragon. Her claws manage to interlock mine, forcing us to fly in small circles as we struggle to stay in the air. Her piercing gold eyes stare directly into mine, full of rage. I fiercely begin biting at their neck, being met with teeth-to-teeth contact as we bite at each other desperately to get the other to release. Our bodies slowly descend back down, struggling to keep each other's weight.

'Hang on, Angel, hang on!' Justin says, putting his hand on one of my spikes. He lets himself dangle as he adjusts his grip. He swings his body backward and uses the momentum to propel himself onto the other dragon. They immediately release their grip, but I tighten mine as Justin slices their head clean off.

"Justin!" I shout, keeping a death grip on its claws as her body goes limp. He tries to hang on but falls from the body as it hangs.

Fueled by panic, I throw the body and dive for him, my claws open wide. His eyes stare into mine, with no hint of fear, as he moves at a dangerously fast pace. My heart pounds as I clasp my claws around his sides, giving a painful lurch of my wings as I stop us only a few feet from the ground.

"That was close. Are you okay?" I ask him as we hover in place.

"I'm fine," he says. I release my grip, making him firmly land on the ground. He smiles before running towards Midnight, who is fighting two minions at once. A wolf suddenly appears from the trees, running fast towards them. My heart leaps with joy as I realize that it is Orion. He leaps on the dragon's back as it duels with Justin, causing it to flip itself around as it struggles to get him off. Justin takes advantage of this and jumps at one of its wings, slicing it clean off. The scream of pain makes everyone pause for a moment.

I start to fly towards them, determined to give Orion my thanks. A wave of nervousness fills me for a moment, making my eyes shift towards the side. Lucifer, still in his human form, is standing to the side of the field, carefully watching the battle take place. I focus my eyes on him as Justin clashes with another dragon, slicing at it with all his strength. It lets out a jet of flames at him, of which he is completely unharmed.

Lucifer gives him a surprised look, staring intently at the small shimmer covering Justin's body. I bank towards his direction and fly as fast as my wings will carry me. A few dragons fly at me but are too slow. Lucifer's eyes meet mine, and he smiles, making my body feel ice cold.

Is this a trap? I ask myself, stopping to land roughly fifty yards in front of him. I look in the direction of Justin, who is now riding on Midnight's back, sword in hand as they slaughter dragon after dragon, Orion close behind them, blood staining his mouth.

"Hello, Angel." His cold voice pulls my gaze back to him. "Why not face me in your true form? Angel, to angel?" he asks, giving me another devilish smile.

"I will not speak to you, Lucifer," I growl, holding my ground.

"Now, now. Make yourself into your human form, and we shall make this quick and painless. We can have a nice chat, it could be rather fun. Otherwise," he looks towards his minions as they land all around us. "You shall face more misery than even you can handle. Then you will truly be mine."

"Angel!" Justin's voice shouts towards me, making my heart sink. All of the dragons flying around us have landed, surrounding Lucifer and me in a large circle. They all stand still, none of them making a sound. Panicked, my eyes meet Lucifer's once more.

"What game is this?" I ask.

"Make yourssself human. I will not ask again," he hisses. I let out a low growl, keeping my place in front of him. In no way will I do what he asks. I have one goal, and that is ending his life. I reach for his mind, wondering what kind of insanity he must be plotting.

Before I can find a way in, the dragons surrounding me open their jaws slightly, releasing a horde of black smoke that creeps towards me. Lucifer grins before turning himself into his massive dragon form. He holds his head high as he watches their smoke creep towards me. I cower in the center, trying to fill Justin's mind with calmness as he struggles to reach me.

'It will be alright; protect Midnight and Orion,' I say to him, closing my eyes and letting myself feel Justin's warmth; my mind drifts to when I slept on his chest. *'I will fight for you. Save yourself...please.*

As the smoke touches my skin, my body falls to the ground, consumed in pain. The connection between Justin and I instantly breaks off as a fiery, pin-needle-like sensation covers my head, making it impossible to move. I think of the strongest walls I can, trying to block them from my mind. The more I try, the more it seems to hurt.

'Give in, Angel. Give in to me, and all will be well...' Lucifer's voice echoes throughout my mind like a serpent made of fire. I feel my body fall onto its knees in my human form.

'I...will...never...' I reply, digging my hands into the dirt. I cocoon myself with my wings making them crystallize into their stronger form, trying desperately to ease the pain. It is as though someone has lit my blood on fire, burning everything from the inside out. A cry out in agony.

'Give in... it will hurt no more...

Tears fall from my face as I continue to fight them, unsure what will happen if I let go. *How could I trust the devil?*

'Give in, and it shall be silent. Trust me.'

The screeching cries of his followers fill my head, piling onto the immense pain holding my body to the ground. Crying repeatedly for me to give in to make the pain go away. I grit my teeth as I let my head hit the ground, barely able to feel it. I let out a long sigh, letting my walls crumble to the ground, my wings softening as I let out another tear.

Silence fills my ears as the pain falls away. I know I am lying on the ground, yet I do not feel or see it. I only see darkness blocking my ears and covering my eyes. But the peace gives me comfort as I let it consume my being, filling my soul in a coldness. My wings tremble as my connection to their magic breaks off.

"Now, show me your true form." Lucifer's voice whispers ever so gently and almost calming in my ears. Unable to feel a thing, my body seems to do what he commands. His satisfied emotion shines through me, the only thing I can handle. "Kill," he whispers once more. The words confuse me; they used to mean evil, but it is calming. My body seems to be moving, following whatever he pointed at, the darkness still covering my sight. As I walk, it is as though my soul is disconnected. The immense power I used to feel was gone entirely.

I try to feel for my wings, but the moment I do, the pain erupts throughout me once more. I close myself off again, relieving the pain instantly. It seemed as though he would not let me feel what was happening.

As my body moves forward, a faint 'clink!' fills my ears, ending the silence. *What was that?* I ask myself, wondering what on Earth would make such a noise amongst all of the dragons. My mind freezes.

'Justin!' I shout to myself, fighting hard at Lucifer and his minion's minds. Fire erupts throughout me once more. I push toward the feeling, determined to detach him from me. The more I fight, the more pain consumes me. His voice fills my ears once more, trying to deter me. I reach for it, finding the source of his connection to my mind. In an instant, I snap at him, cutting off his bridge to my mind.

Within an instant, I let out a gasp as my soul seems to reconnect with my mind, and my eyes are cleared of darkness. The sight below me shatters my heart. My teeth are sunk into a warm neck, the taste of blood filling my mouth. I instantly release, my eyes meeting Justin's. The small glimmer of green that was once in his eyes had faded away. He gives me a weak smile as life leaves his eyes. His armor is completely visible, torn into by my claws, and covered in his blood.

I step off from his body, falling to my human knees. I let out a cry, planting my face into his chest. *My dream, why didn't I listen to my dream?* I think to myself, cradling his lifeless body in my arms. I wrap my wings around him, screaming as I try to let my mind reach his, finding nothing.

I desperately pull a feather from my wing, pushing it onto his chest with both of my hands, trying to reach my power and push it onto him. My head falls backwards as I let out a heart wrenching scream that sends a green shockwave throughout the meadow. All the dragons near me suddenly fall to the ground.

After a few minutes, I sit myself up, all of my grief controlling me as I look around. Lucifer's demons lay all around me, most of them completely lifeless. Lucifer stands back, watching me closely. Midnight is behind me, her leg stuck underneath one of the now dead dragons. I dare not look in her direction. I notice the sword lying a few feet from Justin's body. *He dropped it?* I say to myself, knowing he didn't have the heart to kill me. I stand up, noticing the color of my wings. They are entirely black, all of their whiteness drained away. Emptiness fills me. *I truly am a demon.* Without a second thought, I make my way to the sword. I firmly grasp it, holding it in front of my eyes.

It is beautiful; it shimmers a bright green, shining brightly as all of its enemies' blood has filled it. It lets out a faint hum as though it was calling to me.

"Angel, no!" Midnight screams, fighting to get out from underneath it.

"You're worth more than this!" Orion cries from somewhere behind me. Their voices are like white noise; they mean nothing to me.

I place both hands firmly on its handle, extending my arms out and pointing the tip at my chest. Midnight pulls herself free, rushing towards me. I glance at her, letting the sword sting my chest as I plunge it into myself a moment before she pushes my body to the ground. Her eyes meet mine, tears swelling as she watches my eyes roll back, filling my sight with darkness.

She is cast aside abruptly as claws grasp me, lifting me high into the sky as I bleed out, carrying me far from the battlefield. The sound of giant wings echoes through my ears.

The end.

An Excerpt from Angel: Broken
Coming soon

Chapter One
Chaos

"You're not done yet." An unfamiliar voice echoes, pushing Angel's soul towards a portal with his own hands.

* * *

It was a strange place, full of newness and destruction. I was surrounded in darkness, completely unaware of who I was. My mind was blank, full of a fuzzy sensation. I focused my attention on a pair of pure white eyes that stared into my very soul from across the darkness. A strange force pushed me towards it, calling to me. I slowly reach out to it, my hand trembling. A soft, yet strong, hand suddenly grasps mine, pulling me through a tunnel of some kind.

I catch my breath. *Am I dead?* I think to myself, staring at the ground underneath me. The stranger offers her hand once more, her now light green eyes meeting mine. She looks so different now; she was a shadow, now I see a tall girl before me, covered in armor.

"What is this place?" I ask her, trying to get a good look at my surroundings. Nothing seemed right. *I don't belong here.* I tell myself.

"This is the World of Chaos. I wasn't supposed to look at you, but I couldn't help myself. You are from Earth, correct?" She asks me.

"Earth, that sounds right. But… I am not really sure. I…" I struggle to remember, a fiery sensation filling my head as I think. "I don't know, I must have lost my memory."

"And your wings, what of those? You're not an angel, are you? A demon perhaps?" She questions, staring intently at the wings attached to my back. *I have wings?* I ask myself, completely in shock.

I let myself feel for them, stretching them out in front of me so I have a clearer view. They are white, and every feather has a black tip, making them appear slightly checkered. They are relatively large, the very tips nearly scraping the ground below. I twist my body around, stretching and turning them to get an idea of how they feel.

The bases of them were incredibly muscular, it was clear they were well exercised. The feathers themselves felt delicate, yet powerful. They were full of nerves; I could feel almost every individual feather.

"I didn't realize I had them. They feel strong, I must have used them a great deal." I say to her, continuing to admire their strength and beauty.

"Perhaps I can help you remember. I am Lana, by the way. This is a dangerous land, one that you should not be at for long."

"It is nice to meet you, but I am not sure how you can help me remember. My mind is full of fire and fuzziness. I don't even know my name."

"I won't be able to, but I know someone who can." She says confidently.

"Why would you want to help me?" I ask her.

"I don't really know, to be honest. But something inside me is telling me to. I think we are connected somehow."

"Well, you did pull me out of a... Well, I don't really know what." I say, turning towards the strange maze of mirrors. Her hand quickly turns my head away. "Wha—"

"Don't look at them, you'll just pull more things through. Now, let me take you to my husband. He will be able to help, I am sure of it."

"Is he far?" I ask her, my attention turning towards the vast and barren landscape before us.

"Not at all." She replies, starting to walk towards it.

A tall man comes into view. A mask covers his face and he seems to be surrounded by darkness; the sight of him sends a shiver down my spine. He does not seem pleased to see us coming his way, his eyes meeting Lana's.

"What have you done? She is not supposed to be here." He says in an angry tone, making me take a few steps behind her.

"I couldn't help myself; she was calling to me. I think we are meant to help her. She is lost and broken." Lana places a hand on me, pushing me in front so that the man can see me clearly.

"She is a dream walker," he says rather confidently, slowly approaching my side, taking small steps around me as he looks me up and down. "She is nearly dead, but she is trapped. There is darkness in her, fueled by regret and rage. She must remember who she was, otherwise, she may never be able to escape." I swallow hard, not moving a muscle as he touches my wing. He gently runs a hand through my feathers, making them tingle at his touch. Lana stands beside us, carefully watching him.

"Is she an angel or a demon? I cannot tell." She asks.

"Neither, but she is a God's creation. A weapon of some kind. She's dangerous Lana, you must be careful. Since she is a dream walker, she can't be harmed here. Not without mana." *I am a weapon? A creation? What does this all mean?* I think to myself, running my hands through my hair. His eyes meet mine in an instant, narrowing as he stares intently into my very soul.

"I can try to reach into her with my darkness and try to untangle her thoughts." He suggests, continuing to stare into my eyes. "That is, if that is what you want." I try to look away from his penetrating gaze but seem to be stuck in a frozen state.

"I…I don't know what I want, do as you wish." I whisper to him, barely able to speak.

"Once I enter your mind, and tap into your memories, you will be able to see them as well. You'll see what I see."

"Okay." I reply, closing my eyes as his hands touch my face, his darkness consuming me.

We are standing in a large empty space, surrounded by large steel walls. He seems almost surprised by this. He opens his hands up and snake-like black spikes slither out, exploring the walls around us.

'You have an immensely powerful mind, whatever it is hiding, it does not want me to find.' His voice echoes inside my head. *'Feel our connection, and let me in. Your subconscious is fighting us.'* With his words, I take a hold of his hand and let myself feel his presence. Calmness fills me as we touch, making my mind have a sense of comfort. In an instant, a crack appears inside one of the walls, moving from the bottom to the top as it splits a small hole through it.

The stranger lets his darkness seep through, and it pulls on the barrier more and more, causing the walls to crumble. As he pulls, an image of what appears to be me comes before us.

I am closing my eyes and counting as a small boy runs from me, giggling happily. He crouches behind a small tree.

'Hide and seek?' I ask him, watching as I suddenly transform into an animal. A small, winged cheetah cub now stood before us. The young boy looked terrified at the transformation, and the cub cowered down in response.

We watch as her, my, mother appears, cursing and calling her a "demon" as she abandons her on the side of the road. The image flickers as I seem to be woken up from sleep, as the barrier quickly rebuilds itself once more, briefly sending a sense of pain throughout my mind.

'What happened?' I ask him.

'There's something that your mind is hiding from us,' He lets out a deep breath before sending more of his darkness towards the walls. *'This may hurt a bit, but you can trust me.'*

Memories begin to flood my brain; fragments and images of me transforming into different creatures and growing my powers as my age grows. I seem to favor being a dragon, as I do most of the fighting that way.

None of the memories I am shown are whole, cutting off at random times. We learn that my name is "Angel", and I was trained by a black panther named Midnight. We seem to have had a strong bond that only became stronger as I progressed.

One memory, the most fragmented of all, stands out from the rest. I was fighting a large army, full of a multitude of the devil's followers. The battle skips and sputters throughout, as I tried to make my way towards Lucifer himself. The memory is surrounded in darkness of its own making, as it continuously fights the stranger as he tries to unravel it. I watch in horror as I appear to stab myself with a blade, only for the barrier to become even stronger as we try to pry. Pain shoots throughout my body, causing me to panic. The stranger takes his grip off of me suddenly, causing us both to stumble as we leave my mind.

"I don't understand, everything is so jumbled together, what am I blocking from us?" I sigh, running my fingers through my hair, trying to understand.

"Well, Angel, you could see the amount of training you have. Your mind is powerful, and it does not want us to see what caused the anguish inside of you. We made great progress nevertheless."

"Angel," Lana repeats, staring at me with caring eyes. "It is a beautiful name," Her attention turns towards her husband. "Cobra, could we watch over this one? She is clearly in need." *Cobra.* I repeat to myself.

ANGEL: BROKEN